The Japanese Princess and the American Rebel

by

Carl L. Poston Jr.

DORRANCE PUBLISHING CO., INC.
PITTSBURGH, PENNSYLVANIA 15222

All Rights Reserved
Copyright © 2003 by Carl L. Poston Jr.
No part of this book may be reproduced or transmitted
in any form or by any means, electronic or mechanical,
including photocopying, recording, or by any information
storage and retrieval system without permission in
writing from the publisher.

ISBN # 0-8059-6342-1
Printed in the United States of America

First Printing

For information or to order additional books, please write:
Dorrance Publishing Co., Inc.
701 Smithfield Street
Third Floor
Pittsburgh, Pennsylvania 15222
U.S.A.
1-800-788-7654
Or visit our web site and on-line catalog at www.dorrancepublishing.com

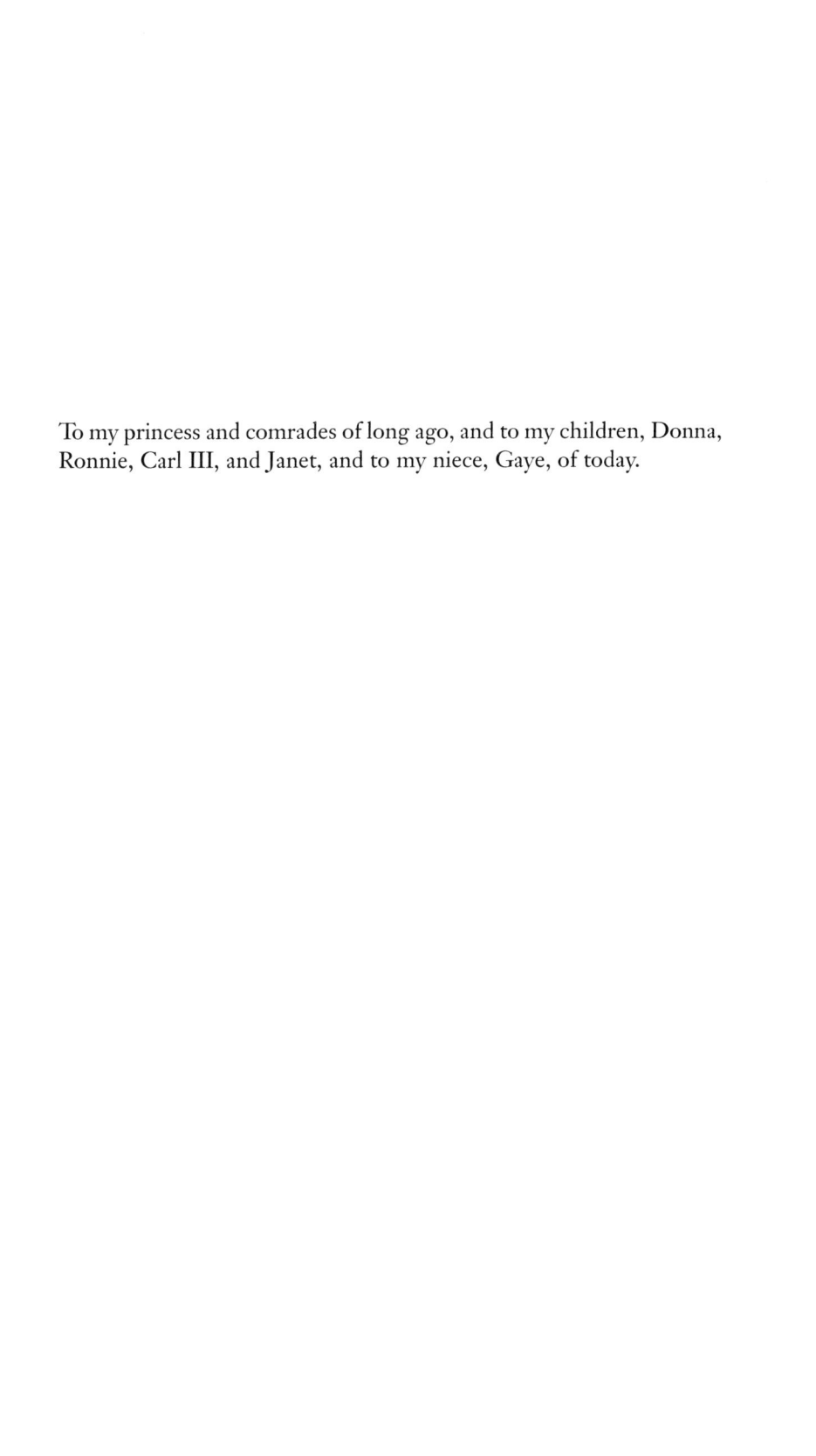

To my princess and comrades of long ago, and to my children, Donna, Ronnie, Carl III, and Janet, and to my niece, Gaye, of today.

Contents

Chapter I   Japanese Princess 1

Chapter II   Korea 33

Chapter III Return To Japan 72

Chapter IV   Afterwards 91

Chapter V   Return To Korea And Home 100

Foreword

It was a long, long time ago, and as our goodbye song "Auld Lang Syne" says, we have truly run about in all directions and wandered many a weary mile while broad seas have roared between us. But, I haven't forgotten my mates of old long ago or the "Land of the Morning Calm" and "The Land of the Rising Sun," where we so closely bonded. Ever so often they come to mind, and I make a toast to each of them.

Here is to you, Dexter, Ben, Ernst, Boy San, G.I. Joe, Mr. Ha, Big York, Buck, James, Terry, Wilson, Hill, Otsu, and especially to you, Namiko, My Beautiful Little Japanese Princess—my beautiful flower and the rich garden from which you grew—the one who taught me the magic of love and the one who is still so much a part of my life. I know the Japanese people are proud to have you as an emblem of their goodness.

Chapter 1
Japanese Princess

I have been here before
    But when or how I cannot tell;
I know the grass beyond the door,
    The sweet keen smell,
The sighing sound, the lights around the shore.
You have been mine before,—
    How long ago I may not know:
But just when at that swallow's soar
    Your neck turned so,
Some veil did fall,—I knew it all of yore.

"Sudden Light"
Dante Gabriel Rossetti
(1828 - 1882)

I first saw her on the island of Eta Jima, Japan. I had overheard the men of my class, as well as other soldiers on base, talk about her. I thought it was unusual for the army to allow such activities on base, but she was doing business at the canteen.

"It's cheap enough," said Whitey. "She only charges two dollars."

"You can't beat that price," added John.

"She sure is a beauty, ain't she?" said Terry.

"She's the best looking Jap I've ever seen."

"She's a beauty in any nationality," added someone else.

"I'd give two dollars just to look at her."

"I went over there yesterday, but the line was so long, so I backed out."

For over a week, I had been hearing such talk about her. Then, Ben Carr had somehow managed to save two dollars and wanted to go see her. That evening I walked to the canteen with him. When we walked in, Ben took a

Carl L. Poston Jr.

place behind five other soldiers who had two dollars each. I looked over, and there she was.

At first, I thought she was a little girl. She was so small, she looked only about four feet ten inches tall and approximately ninety pounds. A thick ponytail hung down her back almost to the chair seat. It was the shiniest black hair I had ever seen, and she had the eyes to match. It took only a second, though, to see that this was no child. Her lips had the perfect curve and a smile to soften the hardest heart. The smile could be seen in her eyes long before it reached her lips. She was dressed in a western style, in a full white blouse and brown skirt just short and tight enough to expose a pretty knee and shapely leg. Without any doubt, she was the most beautiful thing I had ever seen, and I couldn't help but stare. Things kept coming to mind such as "Japanese Doll" and "Japanese Princess."

While standing there watching her, I was suddenly overcome with a strange feeling of having known her. But that could not be, because until three weeks ago, I had never seen a Japanese person. She seemed to sense my stare and turned to look at me. Smiling, she then lowered her sparkling eyes as Japanese women do. That very moment, I felt the sting of Cupid's arrow.

She sat with a pad in her lap while her model sat in front. Then with only a thick lead pencil, she would complete the portrait in a matter of minutes. All around her stood pencil portraits of movie stars such as John Wayne, Marilyn Monroe, Gary Cooper, and others, which she must have done from magazines. Her talent amazed me as much as her beauty.

After the completion of Ben's portrait, I had no reason to stay and stare. So I left with Ben proudly holding his portrait and talking about how his mother would like it. I hardly heard him. My mind was still at the canteen.

I was in Japan on the island of Eta Jima attending a military school. The island is about four miles across the bay from Kure. Until war's end, it had been the Eta Jima Military Academy for training Japanese military officers. After the war, the occupying American army turned it into a specialist school for all branches of the U.S. military as well as British and Australians.

It was a small and very beautiful mountainous island. The hills and peaks left only enough level ground for the school and the small village. The bay waters lapped at the back and on one side of the school grounds, while a mountain wall enclosed the other. Between the school and the village ran an eight-foot high stone fence. It was vine-covered and ran from the bay to the mountain wall, completely separating the school from the village.

The main building of the school was a big three story building constructed of stone and marble. It was very roomy and in the shape of a horseshoe. It was used for living quarters and classrooms. The grounds around the building and down to the bay were landscaped in the Japanese tradition. From the building to the water ran little stone footpaths. Along these paths, and on both sides, grew miniature trees and shrubs about head-high, giving a feeling of privacy. The paths never ran straight for long, but kept to a subtle curve, making one wonder what lay ahead. Ever so often, the path would wander beneath a vine-covered trellis with a seat for two. Here one could sit and listen to the waterfall tumbling into the goldfish pool. From there, several footbridges led over the pools and down to the bay where all paths terminated. At the water's edge, picnic tables and benches were placed about beneath the pines on lush green grass. Here one could sit quietly and relax while listening to the waves washing gently on the shore and the breeze whistling softly through the pines.

On its side of the fence, the school was well equipped for entertaining its students. There were facilities for baseball, basketball, tennis, and swimming. A gym was available, and there was rowing in the bay. There was also a movie theater, and of course the canteen where I had seen her.

On the other side of the fence, the village was tightly pressed down between mountain peaks. Before the Americans came, it was a simple little village of fishermen and farmers, with only their homes and small farming plots. Now, the buildings had expanded to cover every square foot of land as high up the slopes as practical. The new buildings were not for housing the Japanese, but for restaurants, bars, and houses of prostitution, all demanded by the American presence. In fact, this demand made the land too valuable for farming, so the farmers were pushed even further up the slopes. High as could be seen, little plots had been terraced out and planted, and here and there a farmer was seen working the little fields with his big hoe.

For transportation, the island was criss-crossed with foot and bicycle paths, but the only road was made of gravel. It ran three miles from the school, through the village, curving between two peaks and down to the ferry docks. The only vehicles for this short road were a few Japanese taxis and US military vehicles. The US Army also ran a shuttle bus between the school and the ferry for military personnel only.

At the dock were two ferries for trips from the island to Kure. One was a large yacht with about thirty seats arranged on two decks. This yacht belonged to the US Army and transported only military personnel. The other was a Japanese ferry which seated about fifty passengers and four vehicles. Both Japanese and military personnel could ride this ferry for a fee.

The people of the island had lived uninterrupted lives for untold generations, knowing nothing of a foreigner, much less ever seeing one. Then in 1945 they, like all the people of Japan, were completely demoralized when Japan surrendered. All the values and ideals they had lived and died for were gone. Pride of race and country were no more. Their cities lay in rubble and ruin. So many of their young men were sacrificed, all for nothing. Then the horror of it really sank in when the dreaded American Yankees came and occupied their beloved land. We were the first foreign invaders ever to set foot on their sacred soil.

But the people of Japan had something going for them. It was a very powerful thing. It was a thing no invader could take away. It was a dignity, self respect, and discipline that drove them. It drove them, so that in seven years they had rebuilt their torn country and earned their independence, and later stood as an economic power of the world. What a wonderful people!

Back to the American side of the fence: all the many means of entertainment provided by the army just weren't enough to keep the young men in for an evening. The lure and pull of the village was just too great. Things like baseball, movies, and such, would always be with them, but a place like the village of Eta Jima, they had never experienced and would never experience again. So they went out for an evening, like fruit bats from a cave.

The village was waiting with its delicious fruit. Its three streets were lined with restaurants, bars, and houses of entertainment, all full of young, pretty, and cheerful girls. Of course, they didn't have to go into any of the houses of entertainment to meet girls, because the streets were also full. Shortly after stepping through the gate, a young man would be approached from all sides by ladies of the street, each trying to lure him into her house. He soon learned to guard his hat, or one may snatch it and run into her house. He would then have to go in after it or be in trouble for being out of uniform. Once he was in her house, she opened her big bag of tricks to keep him, and as often as not, it worked.

It was sort of a "Cinderella story." The men could have a ball, but if not on base by midnight, bad things would happen to them. At the stroke of midnight, the military police started patrolling, and any soldier found in the village was arrested. So if not on base, he better stay hidden in a girlfriend's house.

However, he had another option. If he didn't want to stop partying at midnight or became bored with the village, he could catch a ferry to the city of Kure. There he would find many more places of entertainment and no curfew.

And of course, the men in my group were regulars at the village and Kure. But the evening after seeing the artist, I didn't go out with them. Instead I went to have my portrait done.

When I arrived, she had no customers, so I walked up and took a seat in front of her. She looked at me and smiled. I hadn't been dreaming. She was beautiful. This day she was wearing a dress of longer length, but with a split that still showed a shapely knee. Her hair wasn't in a ponytail, but hung loose almost covering her back. I soon learned that Japanese women used more hairstyles than American women. One day it would be loose with bangs. The next day it may be tied back in a ponytail or pigtails, or it may be in a high bun full of combs. You never tired of their hairstyles.

"Hi," she said, "you here with friend yesterday."
"Yes," I answered, surprised but very pleased that she remembered.
"He like portrait?" she asked.
"Very much."
"Now you come for portrait?"
"Yes," I said, but thought, *no, I came to look at you.*
"Okay," she said, "turn head little to right."

She then placed the pad in her lap, looked at me and started drawing. Suddenly she stopped, stood up, and stepped toward me. Then reaching out, she took a little curl which always fell on my forehead, wound it tightly around a finger and let it fall. She sat back down and commenced to draw. Her touch had sent my heart racing.

In a matter of minutes, she had finished and handed me the portrait, which I still have. She had even captured the little curl. I looked at it and then back to her beaming face.

"Like?" she asked.
"Oh yes, it's very, very good."
I paid her and then asked, "What is your name?"
"Namiko."

She saw I was having trouble pronouncing it, so she wrote it on a pad in English and handed it to me, while pronouncing it several times. I kept trying until it was pronounced to her satisfaction. Then she broke out in a big smile and nodded excitedly like a dedicated teacher just getting a point across to a dense pupil.

I took the pad and wrote "Carl," and handed it back to her while saying, "Carl."

Later I learned that the letters meant nothing to her, because she couldn't read English. Even though she had learned to speak some English and copy her name in English letters, she still couldn't read or write the language. She tried saying it several times, but had trouble with the "L," because there is no "L" sound in Japanese. It sounded more like "Carr."

"Namiko, you are not busy," I said. "Would you like to go to the cafeteria for a drink and sandwich or something?"

"That be nice," she said, and immediately got up, arranged herself, and we walked over.

We must have sat and talked for an hour. Her English wasn't very good, but it was 100 percent better than my Japanese. However, even with the language barrier, we really seemed to communicate. But if we had been unable to speak a word, I would have been content to sit and gaze at her. Those black sparkling eyes, that smile, that laughter that came forth so easily, the sincere way she seemed to hold to my every word—all those things and more made her so pleasant and easy to be with.

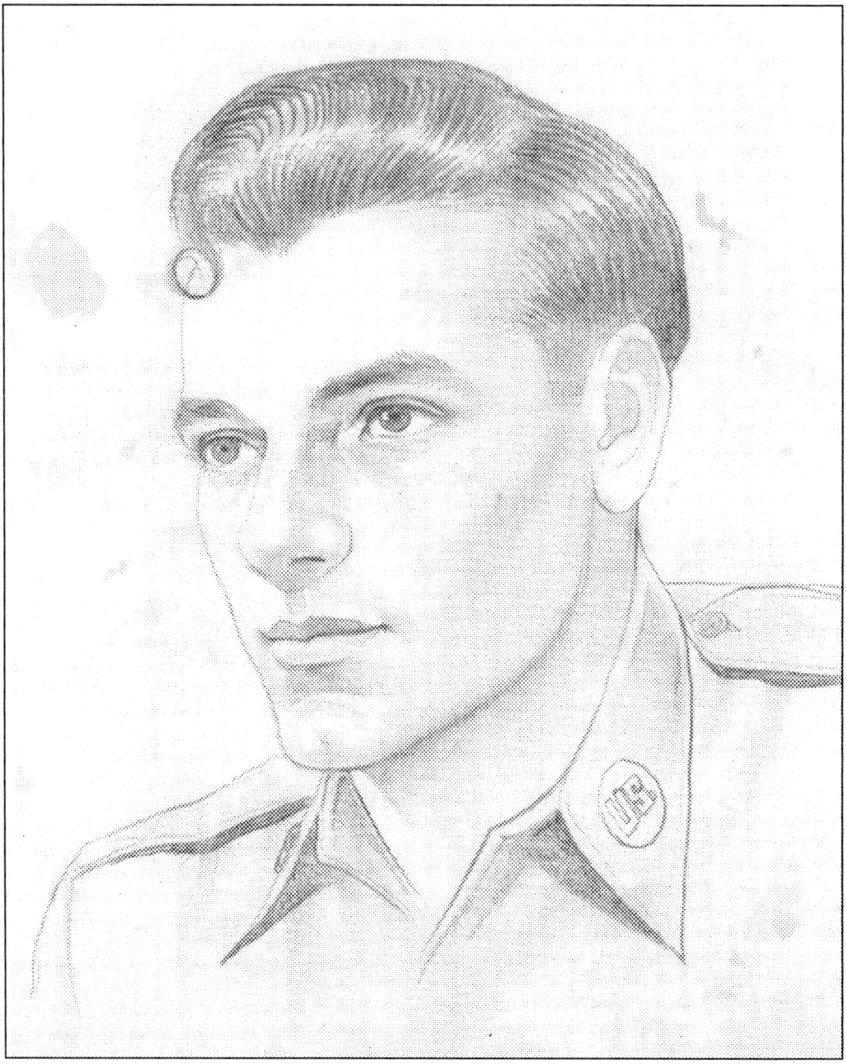
US

In fact, she was so pleasant and easy to speak with, I learned a lot about her in that short time. She was twenty-three years old, but if one counted as Americans count age, she was twenty-three minus nine months, because Japanese are nine months old when born. I was twenty-one. Her mother and two younger sisters were the only members of her immediate family living. Her father and three brothers were killed during the war. She did have many cousins and aunts, but not many male members, which was typical of Japanese families due to so many men killed in the war. She had never been married and had lived all her life in the three places of Hiroshima, Kure, and the island of Eta Jima. She then lived most of the time on the island doing her portraits and helping her aunt and cousin in the Cabana Bar and Restaurant.

When the time came to leave, I told her I had enjoyed the evening and bid her goodnight. She thanked me with a smile and bow and said she had also had a wonderful time, and asked me to come back to see her. I said I surely would and rode all the way to my bunk on a cloud.

The next day was Friday, and we were off duty for the weekend. Our class of eighteen-fifteen Army, two Marines and one Air Force, like everyone else, would go into the village after classes. Most times, we would hang around the village until about ten P.M. and then catch the ferry to Kure. All eighteen of us got along well together, but that is too many people for all to be close friends. So as people always do, we drifted into several little groups. My gang consisted of the following:

Dexter Jackson was from Ohio, and somehow we had been together as buddies since basic training. We had drunk and chased girls together from Alabama to Seattle, Washington, and on to Japan. Ironically, from there, we would go to Korea, back to Japan, then back to Korea, and still be together. And our togetherness wouldn't end there, because we would leave Korea together and spend a short time in San Francisco. There we would part, never again to meet.

Ben Carr was from a small town in Pennsylvania. He was a big beefy fellow with a heart to match. No one was immune from liking him. He was a happy-go-lucky person who could always find something to joke and laugh about, even in the most dire situation. He was a good soldier and earned a few stripes in his career, but always found some way to lose them, and he usually blamed us.

Ernst Berger was born a German citizen but was too young for Hitler's army. After the war, he emigrated to the U.S. and became a citizen just in time to be drafted for the Korean war. He was practical and thrifty, always having money after the rest of us ran out. Ben called him our banker. He was somewhat severe of nature, but ever so often a crack would show in that severity and a real sense of humor would come forth. He was a womanizer, because he regularly wrote to a girlfriend in Germany and one in the U.S.

From all indications, he was engaged to both. Here in Kure, he also had a serious girlfriend, and later he would have one in Korea. He had them well separated, so they weren't likely to bump into each other. How his affairs ended, I don't know. He was a smart chap though, and I am sure he figured it out.

Buck Metts was from Louisville, Kentucky. He was quieter than the rest but fun to be around. He was a true friend in need and deed.

Terry Thompson hailed from Texas. He was our senior in rank and age. He was a corporal and at twenty-five, the old man. The rest of us ranged in age from twenty to twenty-two, except for Don Wilson who was twenty-four. Terry was pleasant, easy going and laughed a lot.

Don Wilson was an Air Force corporal and a party animal. He was the only married man in our gang. Being well over six feet tall and over two hundred pounds made it hard for him to adjust to the little houses, little furniture, and little Japanese women. But he always managed in a good-natured way. He was always ready for a party or a poker game.

That was our gang, and that evening, after taking in the village until seven o'clock, everyone decided to catch the ferry to Kure. That is, everyone except one. I told them to go on, and if I decided to go later, I would be at Otsu's (my Kure girlfriend) house.

As soon as they left for the ferry, I headed to the Cabana Bar. The Cabana was different from others of the village in that it catered to Japanese as well as Americans. The owners would have liked to have kept it strictly as a Japanese restaurant or tea room, as it had been for many years. But the lure of the American soldier's dollar was too great, so they had a Japanese restaurant downstairs and a bar upstairs. It wasn't a law, or a rule, or even intended, but it turned out to be a segregated place, with the quiet sophisticated Japanese clientele downstairs, and the loud half-civilized Americans upstairs. It sort of reminded me of my hometown theater where the blacks had to watch the movie from the balcony. Now I was in the balcony. However, I did cross the line several times by dining downstairs with Namiko. I never knew if it affected her reputation in any way.

Namiko saw me that night as I walked in, and came forward to meet me. She bowed, took my hand, and again hypnotized me with her smile.

"So glad you come," she said, and led me to a table.

"Drink?" She asked.

"Tom Collins," I answered.

As she walked across the floor, it struck me how different she looked, but just as beautiful—beautiful in a different way, beautiful in an exotic way. In fact, the place had an atmosphere of the exotic or far away places. The decorations were more Japanese, and even the bartenders and waitresses were dressed Japanese style. Namiko was even wearing the Japanese kimono with

The Japanese Princess and the American Rebel

her hair in a high bun full of combs. All this and the Japanese music again brought to mind the two terms "Japanese Doll" and "Japanese Princess." It all made me feel far away in a strange, yet familiar world.

She returned shortly with my drink, and upon seeing her and hearing her voice, it seemed as if I knew her from somewhere, but I couldn't quite place where. She brought her cousin to meet me who was also dressed in a bright kimono. Like all Japanese, she was very pleasant, and after our greeting, they left me to my drink.

Japan didn't have jukeboxes like we did in America, so the bars set up record players with speakers. In catering to the Americans, most establishments played western music. But here at the Cabana, it was mostly Japanese music. I sat with my drink, enjoying the Japanese music when suddenly it stopped. Then Glen Miller's "In The Mood" started playing.

Namiko appeared, took my hand and said, "Dance." I couldn't dance. I never had.

So I shook my head saying, "No, no, I can't dance. I don't know how."

"You can," she insisted, "come, I show. Nobody to watch."

I reluctantly got to my feet and followed her to a darker corner, and there I had my first dancing lesson—just one of many things I would learn from her. But the more important lessons would take years to sink in.

She was busy that night, but came by and sat down every chance she got. I enjoyed the drinks, atmosphere, and of course her company, but at eleven-thirty, I told her I had to go before curfew. She followed me to the door, took both my hands, and looked up at me.

"Please come back," she said.

Knowing I had no choice but to come back, I said, "I surely will."

During the next two weeks, I saw her as often as our schedules permitted. We went to the movie on base twice, and bar-hopping with my gang and their girlfriends several times. I would sometimes talk to her at the canteen but seldom went to her bar anymore, because she was usually busy, and I felt that my presence may disturb her work.

However, one Friday night, I did go to her bar about ten o'clock, which gave me less than two hours to stay. After a few drinks and a few dancing lessons, it was time to go. She walked me to the door, and as we stood close together in the dark entrance, she took both my hands in her little ones and squeezed.

Looking up, she said, "Come to canteen tomorrow. I get off work twelve. I bring lunch. We go to bay. Picnic."

Then she reached up and kissed me lightly on the lips.

I met her the next day at noon, and we walked down to the bay. There we sat on the grass, after she had spread the lunch of Japanese dishes complete with chopsticks. She handed me a pair and then began to eat.

"Hey, what am I suppose to do with these?" I asked, while holding up the chopsticks.

"Eat," she answered without looking up.

"How?" I asked.

Then I noticed her cutting her eyes up at me with a mischievous smile before bursting out laughing. She then handed me a knife, fork, and spoon which she had hidden. Such pranks were typical of her. I found her to be very mischievous with an excellent sense of humor. We laughed a lot at nothing and always had a really good time. She always seemed so happy. Everything excited her. She just had a zest for life.

We sat and ate lunch, just enjoying the day. It was warm and breezy. Some distance from the shore, seabirds were flying about the fishing boats.

We were watching them when she said, "When little girl, father fished here. Sometimes take me out."

I watched her as she looked out over the water. The breeze tugged at her long hair and brought a few strands about her face. It had to be the most beautiful face in the world. It seemed to be the face I had dreamed of and longed for all my life. I reached over and took her face in both hands, gently turning her to face me. Then I kissed her lightly on the lips, then the forehead, then each eye and then back to her waiting lips. After separating from the kiss, her hands came up swiftly to my face, and with a little whimper, pulled me down for a second and longer kiss. After separating from that kiss, my hands remained on her face and hers on mine. There we sat with eyes locked, while fingers explored each others' face, eyes, ears, nose, and lips. It was as if we had just discovered each other, or rediscovered each other after a long absence. It all came so easily, so naturally as if we had done it a thousand times.

In a while we turned and sat close together, staring out over the water. Neither of us spoke as we sat there with our thoughts. I was somewhat puzzled over the intensity of my feelings, and I noticed her glancing over at me with a puzzled look.

After a while she took my hand and looking over, said, "I like kiss. You like?"

"I loved it," I replied. "Want to do it again?"

She said nothing, but looked at me smiling while nodding her head up and down. So we did, and her little face beamed with happiness. My spirit soared from the beauty of that day. It still does when I think back on it. I guess we never know when we are making a lifetime memory.

We lay back on the grass, holding hands, and looking up at the few clouds floating by, high in the sky. In such contentment there is no time, so I don't know how long we lay there. Finally Namiko brought me back to the world by suddenly sitting up, all excited like a little girl, saying, "let's go in boat! Come on. Let's go!"

The Japanese Princess and the American Rebel

So I rented a row boat and off we went. I rowed about the shore watching her face full of excitement, and her excitement excited me.

After a while, she pointed to the other side of the bay and said, "Kure."

I looked and could distinguish a pencil line of land, which I thought to be about four or five miles away.

While I looked, she said, "Let's go."

I looked at her flabbergasted.

"What! Row way over there?" I exclaimed, pointing to the far shore.

"No, silly," she said and burst out laughing. "We go on ferry. Plenty time. Please. I introduce you to my mother and friends."

"Silly." Another American word she had picked up.

When docking at Kure, we took a taxi to her mother's house. It stopped at a busy part of the city where the streets were full of shops and people. It seemed to be just as busy and noisy as any other part of the city, and it certainly didn't look look a residential area. After getting out of the taxi, Namiko led me to an old looking gate of wood and iron, which looked to be about eight feet high.

She opened it, stepped through, and said, "Come."

I stepped through behind her, and she pushed the gate closed.

I looked around and saw that we stood in a very charming little garden, completely shut off from the city by a high wall. The city noise disappeared as if turned off by a switch. I followed her along a path of smooth but uneven paving stones until we reached a seat beneath a rustic shelter covered with vines. There she told me to sit, and she would be right back. As I sat there looking over the garden, I couldn't help but compare the construction of that little place to the construction of one in America.

In America a bulldozer would be brought in to clear and level a few acres. Then equipment would be used to dig holes for ponds and the planting of trees. Dump truck loads of dirt would be placed about, and maybe a load of rock for a rock garden. Concrete walkways would be laid and trees and shrubbery planted. Finally, with a few tables and chairs, you have your garden. It's done quickly and with cost kept in mind.

The Japanese don't have the luxury of space as we do. Space for them has been scarce for a thousand years. So they have mastered—no, they have created—the art of space utilization. They do however, seem to have something we don't—time. It can be seen in that little garden, if one looks closely and thinks about the time it must have required.

That little garden, no bigger than two average size American rooms, cut you off from the city's noise, and gave as much privacy as anyone could need. Everything was miniature and so in proportion that it gave the feel of spaciousness. You just knew that every branch on the little trees had been trimmed to perfection. Here no pile of rock had been dumped, but each rock had been held and judged and then placed in the right spot. Even the sand around the rocks had been raked into little waves to represent the seashore. You felt that anything added or anything taken away would make it not right. It would be like deleting or adding words to a beautiful poem.

Before long, Namiko was back and sat beside me. She looked over and took my hand. Looking at me with her face beaming and black eyes shining, she said, "She call us soon."

I could feel her controlled excitement, and I squeezed her hand. We both anxiously sat there looking out over the garden.

To break the silence, I said, "Namiko, who made this garden and who tends to it?"

"My mother. Me."

"I thought you would have something to do with it."

It seemed as if we had been waiting for a long time, when the sound of a gong came.

Then Namiko jumped up rather nervously, saying, "She ready now. Just watch me. Listen. I tell in English how to do. Mother not understand English."

I just nodded, also nervous in not knowing what to expect, or what to say, or how to say it.

She led the way to a small basin with water running into it, which was near the door. There she stopped and rinsed her hands, and I followed suit. The door leading in was about three feet high. There we both sat on the threshold and removed our shoes. Then we swung inside to a small room of about ten square feet. She slid over to a low table and sat on her legs, then motioned for me to do the same.

The floor on which we sat was a smooth shiny mat, bordered with smooth wood of the same color. The walls were of similar material. Except for the little table in front of us and one scroll hanging from a wall, the room was bare. On the table was one vase with one flower, which I knew was fresh, because water drops still clung to it. Three little tea cups sat beside a little tea kettle, and next to them were three saucers with three little cakes in each. That was all the room contained. Here there was definitely no clutter, and the very simplicity and quietness gave the little room charm. So there in its charm, I nervously sat waiting and wondering where her mother was. Later I learned that a host or hostess is never seated before the guests are.

Soon a little lady, dressed in a bright kimono with her hair in a high bun, appeared across the table from us. She was even smaller than Namiko. Her hair was just beginning to gray, and she was a very nice looking lady. She had the features and smiling eyes of Namiko, and from her,

I could see what Namiko would look like in twenty-five or thirty years, and it wasn't bad.

Namiko immediately rose and bowed, and I did the same. After they exchanged a few words, we were again seated. My legs ached. I would never learn to be comfortable sitting on my legs.

From time to time, Mother would glance at me, but only momentarily before casting her eyes down as was customary for women. I watched Namiko closely, and when she picked up her tea cup, I picked up mine. When she bit a tea cake, I bit one. However, it didn't take long to see that a person would have to acquire a taste for the thin bitter tea. The cake however, was no problem to eat, because it had no taste.

After a few sips and a few bites, Namiko said in a low voice, "Say something to Mother. Anything. She not understand English."

Confused, I just stared at her, not certain what she meant. She caught her mother not looking and then mouthed at me, "Say anything."

So I looked at her mother and lied. "Your tea and cake are delicious."

Namiko supposedly translated into Japanese what I said. Then her mother looked at me, bowed, and spoke.

Namiko translated as, "You are most gracious guest to praise my humble tea and cake."

"Say something else," Namiko demanded.

"What should I say?" I asked.

Without waiting she spoke to her mother in Japanese, and then translated what her mother said. It didn't take long for me to realize what Namiko was doing. No matter what I said, she would translate it as the proper formalized etiquette that it should be. In other words, I could say anything I wanted and still be proper in the eyes of her mother.

So when it came my turn to speak, I said, "You have a very beautiful daughter, and I would like very much to kiss her."

Namiko looked at me aghast, with eyes wide. Then after composing herself, she said something to her mother and then translated to me.

Without being probed, I said, "That's not all I would like to do to her."

Leaving me in mid-sentence, she hurriedly translated something to her mother and then back to me.

I completed my sentence with "I would also like to bite her on the neck and her pretty little ear."

Catching her mother not looking, she punched me, and continued translating while biting her lip to keep from laughing. I was really enjoying myself while her mother was being impressed that an uncivilized American could be so courteous in Japanese manners.

We made it through the tea, and I thought her mother to be a most gracious lady. So much of Namiko could be seen in her, and I found myself wishing I could really talk with her. Finally she rose and bid us goodbye, leaving us to ourselves. We stood there looking at each other until Mother was safely gone.

Then Namiko hit me on the shoulder, saying, "Bad, I should beat."

I pulled her to me saying, "I meant it," and took her ear between my teeth.

She squealed, and we stood there holding each other while giggling.

After we sat back down, I asked, "Well what did your mother think? What did she say?"

"She like. She say she not know American so…so…courteous in Japanese way. Say you speak nice and very pretty man too."

"Handsome, not pretty," I corrected.

"What difference? Same thing. Both mean look good."

"Women are pretty. Men are handsome." I said.

"Oh, I see," she said, as her sharp little mind saw an opening for mischievousness. A smile came and then she started her teasing. "Maybe you both. Handsome all over," she said while outlining me with her hands, "but have pretty curl," twisting it around a finger, "and pretty eyes too," she added while gazing into them.

Then just as suddenly, the smile was gone and a serious look filled her eyes. Her lips trembled a little as she asked, "Where is kiss you told Mother I should have?"

Then for a while we were lost in the promised kiss. After the kiss, we sat and talked, but I was still curious.

So, I asked, "What did you really say to your mother when I said I wanted to kiss you and bite your ear?"

Looking down with her mischievous smile, she said, "I only say what you say," then she cut her eyes up at me.

"I'll bet. You are the bad one," I said. "You are devious."

"Devious," she rolled the word around slowly, "please translate."

"In Japanese or English?" I asked.

"Japanese be better, but English I can understand, be okay."

"Okay, it means—let me see, maybe round about, not straight."

"I still no understand."

"Okay, it means not telling the truth."

"Baka shojiki," she replied.

"Please translate."

"In Japanese or English?" She asked, through her laughter.

"In English," I said, "you mischievous and devious person."

"I know mischievous," she said laughing even harder. "Baka shojiki means is foolish to be honest all time. Sometime hurt feeling."

That was the beginning of our fun with word play.

The Japanese Princess and the American Rebel

After we had calmed from our laughter, she got up and said, "I be back in a minute." Then she left the room.

She was back shortly holding a box, and she took a seat close to me. After placing the box on the table, she began taking pictures of family and friends out to show me. I was greatly pleased that she wanted me to know this much of her. But as she went along, I noticed a gloom slowly overshadow her happiness which turned into real sadness.

One of the pictures to bring about this sadness was of a Japanese Army officer. She handed it to me, saying, "Uncle Chunori, Mother's brother."

Then she handed me another one of a young proud looking Japanese Navy officer, while saying, "Nikkan, my brother."

Her eyes filled with tears. I knew that he was dead, because during our first conversation at the canteen, she had told me that her father and all brothers had been killed. So I didn't know what to say. What did come out was a dumb question that I already knew the answer to.

"Killed in the war?" I asked.

"Yes," she whispered, while nodding her head with tear filled eyes. "Both killed. They were, were…you know, shimpu or kamikaze."

"Yes," I said. "I know kamikaze."

The kamikaze was a Japanese pilot who flew his plane, loaded with explosives, into a target such as a ship. Another name for the practice was shimpu, which means, "Divine Wind" and refers to the typhoon which destroyed Emperor Kublai Khan's invasion fleet of the thirteenth century while attempting to invade Japan.

The Japanese were raised from childhood in the "Bushido Warrior Tradition." The code said they must gladly die for emperor and country. There are many cases throughout the war to show that most believed in this, such as suicide banzai attacks and most choosing death over surrender.

However, suicide missions didn't become official policy until late 1944 after things were really going bad for Japan. The Americans had control of sea and air and were creeping closer and closer to the mainland. Japan was drastically short of aircraft, fuel, and pilots. The airplanes weren't nearly as hard to replace as the pilots, because it took lots of fuel and four hundred hours of training to make a pilot. As a result, the inexperienced pilots were shot down almost as fast as they went up. On realizing they could never have a sufficient number of good pilots to compete, and concluding it didn't take a good pilot to fly explosives into an enemy ship, kamikaze became an official policy.

In October 1944, Admiral Onishi began asking for volunteers. There was no shortage of volunteers, so soon the missions were in flight. The army soon took it up, but they didn't ask for volunteers. They just assigned missions.

The navy sent out almost five hundred missions, while the army sent out over seven hundred, which sank one hundred and sixteen American ships and damaged almost two hundred others. That was more damage than had been done in all previous battles combined. This was great encouragement to the Japanese and great concern for the U.S. Navy. But it came too late in the war. The powerful U.S. economy was in full war production and too strong to be stopped. As Admiral Isoruku Yamamoto, after Pearl Harbor had said, "The sleeping giant had been awakened."

Namiko's brother was raised on the island of Eta Jima, just as she was. During his boyhood, he had played over the island and fished the surrounding waters. He went to school in Kure, and when he finished, he came back to the island to graduate from the Japanese Naval Academy. Then as a navy pilot, he left his beloved island to serve his country in the Philippines. That is where he volunteered for Admiral Onishi's kamikaze unit. When his turn came, he, like the ones before him, wrote his last letter home. Then he took off to fly his planeload of explosives into an enemy aircraft carrier.

Namiko laid a letter on the table, and said, "His last letter."

Her Uncle Chunori's story ends in Tokyo where he was stationed as an army pilot. It was the army's duty to protect the homeland from bombing raids. They hadn't been successful, and Japan's cities lay in ruin. It was very frustrating, because like the navy, they were also short of pilots and planes. But their frustration during the early years of bombing was nothing compared to what it became after the American B-29s came into action. The B-29 was called the "flying fortress" because it could take terrible punishment and still keep flying. It was also surrounded with guns and flew in formation to protect other B-29s. About the only time one was in real danger was when it had to fall out of formation for some reason. Then it became like a lone buffalo separated from the herd, and the wolves closed in to bring it down.

Japan had no defense against them, because B-29s flew at 30,000 feet while anti-aircraft shells reached only 23,000 feet. So the big bombers cruised along dropping their bombs while anti-aircraft shells exploded harmlessly below.

The Japanese army sent their fighter planes up to intercept them, but they had trouble reaching that height, and if they did reach it, they didn't perform well. So in helplessness, the "Imperial Army" stripped their fighters of metal sheeting, guns, and everything not essential to flying. Then when the American big bombers came, the fighters were sent above to ram as many as possible. No explosives were even needed, because once a plane was rammed, both would explode and almost disintegrate. Pieces would fall down to the ground from about six miles up, leaving almost nothing to pick up. To the B-29 crews, this had to be most unnerving, especially as the losses mounted. But soon the Americans had bases close enough to Japan so escort fighters could accompany the bombers and shoot down the gunless enemy planes before they reached the B-29s.

The Japanese Princess and the American Rebel

There, over Tokyo, 30,000 feet in the sky, Uncle Chunori made his noble sacrifice.

Can you imagine what heroes these brave young men would be if Japan had won the war? Can you picture the monuments that would be erected in their honor? But to the victor goes the writing of history and the making of heroes.

When I was in Japan, it was much too soon after the war for the Japanese to think much about heroes. They were too busy trying to recuperate from the war. But surely after these many years, they have many monuments honoring such brave young men, something to honor their supreme sacrifice to a lost cause. Being a Southerner and nicknamed "Rebel," I can sympathize with lost causes. I hope there are many monuments in their honor. I do know of one. Of course, it wasn't there when I was, but it is there now. And it is in a very fitting place at the Historical Museum of Eta Jima—the same naval academy from which Nikkan graduated, and the school from which I graduated when I learned of him. It reads as follows:

Kazunarann Sazare Koishi No,
Magokoro O Tsumi Kasanete Zo,
Kuni Was Yas Ukere

Insignificant little pebbles that we are,
The degree of our devotion does not falter,
As for our country we move toward our final rest

After looking at the picture of her uncle and brother, Namiko handed me one with a group of happy looking pre-teenage girls. They were all smiling and dressed in uniforms.

"My class," she said as she pointed herself out.

Then after a long silence, she said, without looking up, "In Hiroshima, they all killed when bomb fall."

She placed the picture down and picked up another. This one was of a young Japanese couple (the woman looked like Namiko) with three young sons and three young daughters.

"My family," she whispered, "father and all brothers dead." Until then, I never knew she was in Hiroshima when the atomic bomb was dropped. To tell this part of her story, I have put together the things she told me with the things I already knew and the things I later learned.

The city of Hiroshima is on the coast of Japan's Inland Sea where the Ota River empties. It is built on the many islands formed where the river and the sea meet, and its parts are connected by many bridges. In 1945, the city had a population of over 320,000. There the people had been spared from the devastating bombing raids of Tokyo and other cities. They had experienced only a few incidents of the war. One time a few people had been killed when a bomb fell in the harbor. Another time, a B-24 was shot down and the crew captured.

Because it had received no damage from bombing was precisely the reason it was picked for the atomic bomb. Since the city had no damage from past bombing, the explosion would give Japan a good picture of how destructive the new weapon was and encourage her to surrender.

Namiko's father was from the island of Eta Jima, and her mother was from Kure. There the family had two homes, one in Kure and one on the island. That is where she lived until her father went into the army and was stationed at Hiroshima. Then in 1941 when she was nine, her father moved the family to Hiroshima to be near him. She had a big family of three older brothers and two younger sisters. However, by then her older brother Nikkan, was already a navy pilot stationed in the Philippines.

That is why Namiko was in Hiroshima that fateful day of August 6, 1945. It was a beautiful morning as people were going about their business. The buses and street cars were running. People were going to and from work. The streets were filled with thousands of uniformed school children laughing and talking on their way to classes. At the Hiroshima Castle, her father, along with other soldiers were going about their military duties. The American prisoners of war, recently shot down, sat in their cells in this same castle. It was just another day in the busy city to the 320,000 residents.

Namiko's family lived on the edge of the city towards the docks. Her brothers, age seventeen and fifteen, were among the school children. Her oldest brother, Nikkan, had been dead for over a year. That day it so happened that her mother and two sisters, age ten and seven, were ill and she stayed home to care for them. She was thirteen. Later, her sister Isora began feeling better and started to go to school.

While all those activities were going on throughout the city, at 8:20 A.M., almost in the center of the city, close to the castle, a gigantic explosion went off in the air. The heat from the explosion was so great that anyone outside and within a quarter of a mile of the explosion was vaporized. They were no more. There were no remains. Farther out, people and animals caught fire and were gone in a flash. Some left a carbon outline of what they had been. And farther out, people's flesh burned away, leaving their bones as charcoal. Those were the lucky ones, because still farther out, many people had their skin and flesh blown off and hanging in strips. Thousands of people walked around in this condition, not knowing what to do or where to go. Many burned to death, unable to get out of buildings. The American prisoners in the castle were among the victims.

In just a few seconds, that blast killed over 80,000 people. Twenty to twenty-five thousand people died later. Not to belittle the tragedies of today, such as plane crashes and school shootings, but compare them to this. The number killed in this blast is equivalent to three times the population of Florence, South Carolina, the county seat. It is like killing the population of my home town thirty-five times.

Most of the buildings were destroyed leaving little shelter in the city. Many survivors went into the hills around the city where many more died. Some surviving the blast later died from radiation.

At the edge of the city, Namiko, her mother, and her sister Tokiko heard and felt the blast, and even experienced the bright flash in the house. They of course, had no idea what caused it, and wouldn't know for several days. They were not hurt, and even their house escaped real damage. However, they were greatly concerned over her father, brothers, and sister Isora, who had left late for school. So all three started into the city in search of them. But it wasn't long before they realized the search was futile. There were no familiar signs. The fire was everywhere. Smoke and dust were so thick they couldn't have seen any signs if there had been any. The farther they went, the greater the horrors of mangled people became.

Nothing was ever found of her father or brothers. However, Isora was reunited with them the next day. She was alive but badly burned. Even her clothes and hair had been burned away. The family of four males and four females was now a family of only four females. However, the shortage of men in families weren't unusual because before war's end over one and one-half million men would be killed.

Some months later, the mother moved back to Kure with her three daughters. She moved back with half a family.

A few days after Namiko had been searching for her family, and finding only the horror of her neighbors and friends cooked to death and blown apart, on the other side of the world, I was a twelve year-old-boy laying on the floor of our old house in Timmonsville. I lay there listening to Mama as she read from a newspaper about a new type of bomb that had been dropped on a big city in Japan, completely destroying it. Everyone around me was happy and jubilant. Joy and celebration was everywhere. And I probably went back outside, and in my play, continued to kill the dirty little Japs as I had been doing throughout the war, thinking they all should be wiped from the face of the earth.

In Washington, DC and Los Alamos (the birth place of the monster bomb), there was also jubilation. When the scientists and military received intelligence that over 100,000 people had been killed in the blast, there was a big celebration at the La Fonda Hotel in Santa Fe. There were some, though, who didn't feel like celebrating the carnage. Some scientists didn't attend, and one was seen throwing up after hearing the news.

Whether it was necessary to drop this terrible bomb is still debated and will never be settled to the satisfaction of both schools of thought. One argument is that it would have taken 500,000 allied casualties to have conquered the mainland. The opposing view is Japan was close to surrendering anyway. I suppose I concur with Truman's decision to use this weapon, but what I find hard to support is the dropping of the second bomb on Nagasaki a few days later.

It tore at my heart to see Namiko in this state of sadness, especially after never seeing her in any way other than smiling and laughing. Out of this sympathy, I reached over and squeezed her hand. She looked up through tear-filled eyes, attempting to smile. Then she began wiping at her tears and said, "Sorry."

Knowing she definitely had no reason to be sorry, but not knowing what to say, I reached over and kissed the top of her head. I had an urge to just hold her and kiss the tears away, and in some way drive the sadness from her heart. Then almost as soon as the sadness had come, it was gone, and she was again her smiling self. I would have liked to believe that it had been my hug and kiss that brought this about. But I knew better. I knew there had to be a self-sufficiency about her, an inner strength that enabled her to overcome the horrors she had seen.

I sat there for a while looking at this marvelous little woman, summarizing what she had been through. She knew her older brother, her hero, had flown his planeload of explosives into an enemy ship. She had witnessed her city completely destroyed in a single blast. She had seen the mountains of dead, many of them her friends and relatives, shoved into a common grave. From this same blast her father and brothers were vaporized, and her sister severely injured. And then she watched as the feared Americans came in and occupied her country, even taking over her beloved island. Yet through all this, her little spirit shined so brightly. Now she was telling the enemy the story of her life, and winning his sympathy and his love. It amazed me that she could do this, and I wondered how! How could she go through those horrors and not hate the Americans, not hate me, not hate the whole world for that matter? It was such a big question in my mind, I had to ask.

I looked her in the eyes and asked, "How? How in the world can you not hate me and all Americans, and for that matter, all the world?"

Looking at me intently, without batting a eye, and with no hesitation whatsoever, she said, "For long time I did. I hate everything. I even hate me because I live." She went on slowly as she searched for English words. "Hard to explain. English not serve me well. But let's see—I learn from Zen. Fill mind with good thoughts and soon they push bad thoughts out. Bad thoughts never go forever, but gone most time. Zen fill heart with love. Leave little room for hate. Also learn life darkness and light. When we go into darkness, if"... seemingly confused with the language, she stopped the sentence and asked me, "What English word when you wait and wait and when you believe?"

I puzzled over that question and then it came to me. "Patience and faith," I answered.

"Yes," she said and started her sentence again. "Life both, darkness and light, so have to go into darkness sometime. But when in darkness, patience and faith do until light back."

"Honey, you have had your share of darkness."

"I have share of lightness too," she replied.

From the short while I had known her, she often amazed me. This time she left me almost speechless. I did, however, manage one more question.

"What about your mother and sisters, how do they feel?"

"For rest of day let's fill mind with happy thoughts," was her answer.

And we did. She wanted to show me the neighborhood, so we set out walking. Most everyone seemed to know and greet her, especially the children, who ran up to meet her. As we walked along, she would point out certain places and buildings and try explaining them to me. I couldn't have had a better tour guide. She showed me a Christian church. It surprised me to know there were enough Christians in Kure to have a church. She pointed out the temple of Zen Buddhism which was so important to her and her family. Close to the temple was an art gallery.

On pointing that out, she surprised me again by saying, "I have painting there. If was open I show you."

"You have a painting in the art gallery?" I exclaimed.

"Yes, two," she said while holding up two fingers.

Was she always full of surprises.

After touring the neighborhood, she asked, "Hungry?"

"Starving. Those little cakes and tea didn't last long."

She rewarded me with her beautiful laugh, and said, "Come, we find something."

Then she led me to a restaurant where I had to sit on my legs again. She of course did the ordering of the Japanese dishes, and I found the food delicious. With the meal we had saki, which is a Japanese rice wine served warm. I had already experienced saki, and before I was through with Japan, I learned to rather like it.

It had been such an interesting day I was sorry to see the time come to an end. But it did, and we caught a late Japanese ferry, hoping it would allow me enough time to be on base before curfew. There were few people on the ferry, so we sat alone on the back watching moonbeams sparkle across the water. It was a beautiful clear night, with a bright almost full-moon. The bay breeze kept the night cool and pleasant. We sat close holding hands, just enjoying the night and each other, and without being aware of it, making another lifetime memory.

Over the hum of the diesel engines, she said, "I sorry to speak of unhappy things and maybe ruin day."

"Well, let me tell you one thing," I replied. "You certainly didn't ruin our day, because it has been the best day of my life."

"Really?" she asked, quickly looking up at me.

"Yes, really, and I mean the best day of my entire life, but why did you want to tell me?"

"I don't know, I just want to."

"Well, I'm glad you did," I replied.

"Why?"

"Why? Because I want to know everything about you."

"Really?" She asked again and squirmed closer.

"Okay, now tell me about you," she demanded.

"There is little to tell about me."

"How about family, mother, father, brother, sister, and maybe girlfriend. No don't tell me about girlfriend."

I laughed at her, and said, "There's no girlfriend."

"Then family."

"Well, my mother has been dead for a long time. When I was twelve years old she died. My father died about a year ago."

"So sorry," she said with all sincerity.

I told her a little of the rest of my family and then asked, "Why did you want to know?"

"Because," she said, while looking up at me with a big grin. "I want to know everything about you."

As she spoke, I looked at her and was overcome by the beauty of that teasing little princess in the moonlight. I reached and kissed her. It was a kiss that we both were reluctant to let go. Her little face was beaming as she snuggled closer.

I then said to her, "You are my beautiful little Japanese Princess."

"I not a princess," she said.

"Oh, yes, you are," I said, putting a finger on her nose. "You are my princess, you are little, you are beautiful, and you are Japanese. Therefore, you are My Beautiful Little Japanese Princess. Well, maybe not mine, but anyway, Beautiful Little Japanese Princess."

With a big smile, she said, "I like," and reached up and kissed me. "But keep 'my' with it, please."

Then we sat quietly for a long while.

After that long while, she said, "Now I must give you name. Let's see, you my Big Beautiful American Yankee."

Laughing, I said, "Men aren't beautiful. Some may be handsome but not beautiful. Women are beautiful. Some are anyway. Like you. But none are nearly as beautiful."

"Oh no," she said laughing out loud, "Here go again with handsome, beautiful, and pretty. Why not just say man and woman look good. Make

The Japanese Princess and the American Rebel

much more easy."

It was a while before either of us could speak because of the laughing.

Then I continued, "Now that we have it settled that I am not beautiful, I am also not a Yankee. I am from the southern part of the United States. A place called South Carolina. At one time the South and the North fought a war. I am a Rebel and we fought the Yankees of the north. Ben and Dexter are Yankees."

"Yes," she said, "that is what they call you sometime, Rebel."

"Yes," I said, "and I am not big. I only weigh 145 pounds. Ben and Dexter are big."

She pondered that for a while, and then asked, "You fight Ben and Dexter, yet still friends?"

"We didn't fight. The war was a long time ago. Maybe our great-great grandfathers did, but it was long before we were born. Understand?"

"I think so," she answered.

Then after a short silence, she said, "Okay, you help."

"I would like anything you called me, but let's see. How about really, really handsome American Rebel?"

She pulled her legs up, crossed them and sat in the yoga position close to me. She then leaned on me and started her teasing.

Looking up at me while twirling a piece of my hair about her finger, she said, "I think about. But I still think maybe you all three, handsome, pretty, and now beautiful," stressing the last word as she broke out in a smile.

"And you are mischievous and devious," I said.

She said the words mischievous and devious several times. "I like sound, feel good in mouth."

"Maybe I should change your name to Beautiful Mischievous Devious Imp."

"Imp. What Imp?"

"A demon. A devil."

She bolted up straight with eyes wide and exclaimed, "Devil!" Then she burst out in such a loud laugh the few passengers turned to see what was going on between the girl and the American soldier.

Her loud and infectious laugh had me laughing with her. Between her laughing spasms, she said, "Now I devil too."

"Come here," I said, pulling her to me, "this beautiful man wants to kiss the handsome little devil." Our laughter stopped, and with the kiss we both knew.

Then the ferry docked. We got off and took a taxi to the village. At her house I kissed her goodnight and by 11:30, I was in my bunk. I lay there for a long time with the events of one of the most exciting days of my life whirling through my mind, and thinking of the most exciting girl I had ever met or had ever hoped to meet. Finally a restful sleep came, disturbed only by pleasant dreams.

The next night we went to the movie on base. It turned out to be such a lovely full moon night that after the movie we decided to go for a walk in the gardens. The bright moon painted everything in a soft glow, even the little goldfish in the pools and the fragrant flowers around them. The only sounds were the splash of little waterfalls and our footsteps as we walked along the path and over the little bamboo bridges. We said nothing. Talk would have been an intrusion. The night was saying it all.

As we walked along holding hands, engulfed in and entranced by the beauty of the night, I wondered how many Japanese officers had walked these same paths. It had been only a few years back that they were here. They were here holding the hands of their young ladies, speaking of their dreams and their love, all of which was to come after the war, all to come after bringing honor to themselves and to their country. Now where were their dreams, their love, and their honor? I knew not, but I did know that their bones lay scattered throughout the jungles and ocean depths of the Pacific, while their conquerors walked these paths holding the hands of their young ladies.

When we came to the bay, we stood looking out over it toward Kure. In the distance the city's lights shined softly. On the bay a light flickered here and there from a fisherman's lantern. The moonbeams fell about us bringing out the shine in Namiko's hair and eyes. The only sounds were the waves washing the beach and the light breeze whispering messages through the pines. One was a sad message, a sad message of the ones here before and now gone. The other was a happy message, a happy message of dreams and love for the ones here now. We stood there in silence listening to the messages.

Finally the silence was broken when Namiko said, "I think about it."

"Think about what?" I asked.

"What to name you," she replied. "My aunt help me look at words, handsome, beautiful, and your 1861 war. So I decide, 'My Beautiful Big American Rebel.' 'My' because I like to think you mine. Handsome yes, very handsome, but more beautiful than handsome, because you fill my heart with beauty. Body maybe not big like other Americans, but big because you big in my heart. You are American. You are Rebel. So, My Beautiful Big American Rebel…I love you."

Looking down at the most beautiful face I had ever seen, and definitely the face of a princess, I said, "My Beautiful Little Japanese Princess, I love you too."

There we stood embracing, two lovers beneath a full moon in a fragrant Japanese garden. We were two lovers born and raised on opposite sides of the world with vastly different cultures. We were two lovers of different races and countries that until a few years ago were in deadly war. One was from the conquered country, one was from the conquering country, but none of that mattered. Our differences paled in comparison to the love binding us.

Nothing was important but our closeness after we declared our love for each other and feeling our very souls melt into one. I knew then that no matter how far I may go or how long I may live, I would never be free of this woman.

With her head on my chest, she whispered softly, "Stay with me tonight."

I did stay that night and every other night I could.

I have always been an early riser, but that morning, Namiko was up with breakfast and tea before I awoke. She sat it down by the bed and lay down, snuggling close.

Then she asked, "Hungry?"

I nodded my sleepy head.

Suddenly her smile was gone and tears welled up in her eyes.

Then she whispered, "Now we really belong. You are really mine, and I am really yours."

"Yes, we do, and yes, I am, and yes, you are," I replied, pulling her even closer, and burying my face in her hair.

I loved the smell of her hair. I loved the smell of her. She never smelled of powder or perfume, but more of soap and clean laundry, or fresh air after a spring shower. She just smelled clean. The Japanese are well-known for their cleanliness, and she must have been the cleanest of all of them. I don't know that she ever used makeup.

We lay that way for a long time, not talking, not really thinking, but just feeling the pleasure and beauty of being together. It was the feeling of closeness that comes only to two lovers, having declared their love, and then giving everything, gladly giving hearts and bodies and souls for the pleasure of the other.

When we did get around to breakfast, it was cold, but that didn't matter. We could always fix another breakfast. Besides, it would be several days before I had much interest in food or anything else but her.

After that night, it was such torture to be apart, she rented an apartment in the village. I paid for it, because she couldn't afford it. At the time, Japan was still rebuilding its economy from the war. Times were hard for most people, including Namiko's family. That is why she worked two jobs—the bar and drawing portraits at the canteen. Money was no problem for me, because I was a rich American soldier. My monthly income of one-hundred and thirty dollars went far in Japan. Why, I could have supported a big Japanese family on that. Aware of her financial difficulties, I often tried giving her money, but she would seldom take any.

Sometimes she would take part, saying, "This will do."

As long as I have a memory, our little apartment will be in it. It was the typical little one-room Japanese apartment. Of course, it wasn't little by Japanese standards, because most families lived in one to three rooms. It had no shower or indoor toilet, most places didn't. Instead of a shower it had the standard hot-tub, which was an upright wooden barrel with a built in seat. Upon getting in and sitting down, hot water would come up to your neck. I do mean hot. Scalding is a better word for it. Upon coming out, you would be pink like a cooked lobster. Namiko got the biggest laughs out of me trying to get use to being scalded. She would laugh until she couldn't speak. The scalding didn't bother her a bit though. She would jump right in still laughing.

Then she would look at me and say, "See, easy."

Due to the crowded conditions they live in, the Japanese have learned to improvise for their privacy. It always amazed me to see how Namiko could arrange this in our one room apartment. With nothing but a towel, she could so artfully screen herself in bathing and dressing so that I seldom saw more than a towel. Even on beaches where bath houses were non-existent, I had noticed the crowds dressing and undressing the same way. When it comes to the human body, they don't seem to be overly modest anyway, because Japan then had and probably still has public bathing. The people were bathing and talking, but nobody seemed to notice nudity.

I met most of her family and had tea with her mother two more times. But somehow I always missed seeing her sisters. They were always somewhere else. I learned that the Cabana Bar and Restaurant was owned by her Uncle Yoshiya and Aunt Mitchie. Aunt Mitchie was her mother's younger sister. She was thirty-eight years old, and I thought real good looking to be so old. She and Uncle Yoshiya both had spent lots of time in the United States, and both spoke much better English than I did.

Uncle Yoshiya was always nice and courteous, but I always had the feeling that he would love to be slipping a knife between my ribs while bowing and smiling. My feelings turned out to be true, because he was seriously against our relationship. Being the oldest surviving male of the family, his word was almost law in the male dominated society.

Now Mitchie, I learned to love. She was so like Namiko, and they loved each other dearly. She was probably the only one of the family in sympathy with us. Living in and being educated in the United States gave her an outlook that the others didn't have. This should have applied to Uncle Yoshiya, but he was a man, and I was the hated invader.

Aunt Mitchie even accompanied Namiko and me to numerous events in Kure. We went to several plays and a puppet show. The puppets, however, were not like our little puppets on a string or hand-held, but were life size. Mitchie, being fluent in English, always explained the plays beforehand, so I could better understand them. She was knowledgeable on many things, and was one of the most interesting people I have ever spoken with.

On one of these trips, we went to the Buddhist Temple. To me, one of the most memorable things there was a garden. At first glance, I thought it to be under construction and incomplete. It only had white smooth sand with a few rough rocks scattered about. There wasn't much to it, yet it held a fascination for me. I expressed this to Namiko and Mitchie. Then Namiko started speaking excitedly in Japanese, and Aunt Mitchie translated as follows:

It illustrates the simplicity and purity that lie at the heart of Zen. The sand, clean, and pure, and vast, represents Zen. The few rocks, hard and uneven, represent life. Upon leaving the rocks, we are back in the purity and evenness of the sand. In time, even the rocks become sand. In that smoothness and purity, there is no clutter, no distractions. Only peace."

Simplicity. No clutter. No distractions. I then saw how Zen Buddhism had so influenced Namiko. It was in her housekeeping. Neat, orderly, and no clutter. It was in her painting. It was in our relationship. It was in her everything, and the simple beauty shined so brightly in her.

That same day we visited the art gallery, mainly to see Namiko's two paintings. I understood nothing of painting and still don't, but in her paintings, the simplicity and peace of Zen seemed so obvious that I mentioned it.

"You are right," Mitchie said. "Namiko's painting is very much influenced by Zen, as is her life."

That night after our visit to the temple, I lay awake. The garden and strange statues wouldn't leave my mind. One of the statues was especially puzzling. It was of a couple in an obvious sexual embrace. Surely I must be misreading the meaning or symbol of the statue, because no church I had ever been in would allow a sex symbol of any kind to be displayed. Sex was taboo and was only mentioned as the original sin. So I put the question to Namiko. She seemed to understand my question, and even though I couldn't see her face in the dark, I knew she was looking toward me, smiling as she snuggled close. She reached and caressed my face until finding my lips and then placed a kiss on them.

With a little laugh, she said, "You Americans have way of answering question with 'yes' and 'no.' This yes and no question. Yes it about sex, and no it not about sex."

"Well that answers my question," I said. "That was easy and simple enough."

"No, you wait. I not through," she said laughing. "It is sex, but more about Zen. Let's see, maybe I explain this way. Listen and maybe you help with words. Okay. When we, you and me together make love, my thoughts not on me but on you. Don't want anything but you. Want to give myself to you always. I not think what please me but what please you. I not need to think of me, because you think of me. You do same for me as I do for you. So we both become very, very happy because we think of each other and not self. We could not be so happy if I think of me and you think of you. So in those moments of giving, we become one and not two. That not Zen but it very close. Especially in climax, when impossible to think of anything but pleasing other."

She waited a while before continuing.

Then she said, "When speak of sex, I not mean like soldiers pay street girls. That not same. Maybe okay for them, but not same. What I speak of is sex with love, like we and many more people have. So, since so many people experience sex with love, it good way to show path to Zen. It show that to have happiness in Zen, people must forget themselves and make others happy. People must lose themselves in Zen as do in sex. Then they become one with Zen. That is meaning. Understand?"

"Yes, I do," I said, as a teacher of two thousand years ago came to mind with such teachings as "do unto others as you would have them do unto you," and "you first must lose your soul to gain your soul."

Then I said, "Little Princess, you need no help with words," and pulled her closer. Then we became one and not two.

She loved walking along the shore and collecting shells, or more like looking at them because she seldom kept any. If one got her attention, she would pick it up and examine it closely and then place it back in the spot she found it.

I became acutely aware of this one day when I had picked a shell up, glanced at it, and threw it down.

"No," she said, picking it up and placing it back where she thought I had found it. "Should go back in same place. Belong there."

"Why? The waves will just wash it someplace else."

Reaching and putting her arm through mine as we walked along, she said, "Ocean know much better than we where shell should be."

I had never known anyone so sensitive in not disturbing the nature of things as she was, nor would I ever. She was an environmentalist when environmentalism wasn't cool. She would examine a flower in the same way she did a shell and then leave it alone. One day near her waterfall, we came across a patch of wild flowers. She immediately fell on her knees and began fondling the flowers and almost examining them one-by-one.

I noticed one I thought to be especially pretty and reached to break it off, saying, "This will look nice in your hair."

"No." She stopped me. "Too pretty to die so soon. Leave to show beauty longer."

"Show to whom?" I asked. "Nobody comes here."

"Maybe other flowers," was her answer.

Walking along the beach, I said, "Namiko you seldom save any shells. What kind are you looking for?"

"Seashell of forgetfulness," she answered.

"What does it look like?"

"I don't know," she replied.

"You don't know? How will you know if you find it?"

"Because of what it does."

"What does it do?" I asked.

"It makes you forget things."

"Do what?"

"Yes, that is why it is named the seashell of forgetfulness. It makes you forget things," she said.

I wasn't certain whether she was pulling my leg or what, but anyway, I asked, "How does it work?"

"You think unhappy thoughts and hold shell close to heart and puff, you forget. Bad thought gone. Never return."

I was beginning to notice an impish look on her face.

"Aw come on, you don't really believe that," I said. "Do you know of anyone ever finding one?"

"No, but they are so few to find because they come from far away."

"Where do they come from?" I asked.

"They wash down from a river far, far away, and few of them ever reach the ocean beaches."

"What's the name of this river?"

"It's the River of Forgetfulness where all souls must gather before taking up new lives. Once they drink from this river their prior lives are forgotten and they enter their new lives unburdened with past memories."

I burst out laughing. "And where is this river?"

Then it was her turn to burst out in laughter. "No one knows. If they find, they forget."

She was always full of entertaining stories.

"Why do you want to find this shell," I asked, "to forget me?"

She stopped, reached up and kissed me, saying, "No, it wouldn't be strong enough for that."

We walked along for a while in silence.

Then she broke out laughing and said, "Maybe need two shells."

I grabbed her and pulled her to me, saying, "Come here you little devilish imp."

"Now you call me devil again," she said between peals of laughter.

We both enjoyed my gang and our trips with Mitchie, but as time for my departure to Korea drew near, we preferred more and more to be alone together. There seemed to be a completeness in our relationship that had little need for other people. Regardless of the language barrier, we had little trouble communicating. It was almost as if we could read the thoughts, moods, and needs of the other. I once read of a French trapper and his Flathead Indian wife, who had lived together for over thirty years, communicated perfectly, and neither could speak the language of the other. I could now believe it.

So in the last days of my stay in the Land of the Rising Sun, I seldom went out with the gang. I am sure they understood, but understanding didn't stop them from ribbing me. Until this day, I can still see and hear them as if it were yesterday.

Ben Carr coming up and putting his big arm around my shoulder, while asking, "Going out with us tonight, Reb?"

"No, not tonight. I can't," I replied.

"Why not? Ain't you ever going out with us again? Are you going to let one teeny weeny chick keep you from enjoying all the other girls of Japan?"

Then looking me in the eye and lowering his voice just low enough so everyone could hear, "Hey, Reb, I got an idea. She is small enough, so why not hide her in your duffle bag and take her with you to Korea?"

Then turning to the others, winking, and saying, "Boys, this is a case of true love and it's time we showed it more respect."

Ernst cutting in with his German accent, saying, "Ben, you wouldn't know love if it hit you in the face. The only love you know and the brain you have is in your pecker. Wherever it leads, you go."

Ben looking down and saying, "Lead on brain." Then looking back at me, saying for everyone's benefit, "It has to be love, because there can't be any screwing going on. She is too little for that."

"Hmph," adding Dexter, "She's as big as a fist isn't she?"

Everybody laughed.

Then Terry in his Texas drawl coming in, "I'll tell ya one thang, you better not let that mean fiery Otsu in Kure run into ya. She asked about ya the other night, and I told her you were busy. She said 'busy bullshit, I know bastard busy with some whore.' And don't forget that butcher knife we took from her. She may have another and not only threaten to cut it off."

"Let me get away from you barbarians and see if I can find some civilized people," I said.

As I was leaving, Ben got them going in a sing-song, "Reb is in love, Reb is in love. Love is going to rob Reb of all the other nookie in Japan."

Late one night with only a few days of my stay in Japan left, I lay awake hugged tightly to her back. I lay still, feeling the beat of her heart and listening to her soft breathing. I was thinking that in a few days, I wouldn't have her like this, and God, how I would miss her. I wondered how it ever happened that I came to need and want someone as I did her. I had never before felt this way about anyone. I had liked a few girls, maybe felt a little love, but all that put together was nothing compared to this.

As I lay there thinking, something aroused her probably my intense feelings, and she turned to face me.

She put her little arms around my neck, and without opening her eyes, asked, "No sleep?"

"No," I replied. "I was just thinking how much I am going to miss you, and wondering how anyone can love as much as I love you. I think I loved you from the first time I saw you."

"That easy question," she replied sleepily, and still not opening her eyes. "I love you just same. No one-life time love. You know carnation?"

"No," I answered.

"You know," she said. "How say carnation, migrate?"

I puzzled over that for a few moments, and then asked, "you mean reincarnation or migration of souls?"

"Yes," she smiled and opened her eyes wide. "Our souls always love. I know in my heart. I not know first time we meet, but day we picnic on beach and kiss, I begin to know. And after ride on ferry that night, I know for sure. I know then we belong this life, all life."

She then kissed me and said, "Now go sleep," and almost immediately she was in a deep peaceful sleep, leaving me with my puzzling thoughts.

When our goodbye came, it wasn't so bad because we had prepared ourselves. We knew that if nothing drastic happened, I could return in six months. Shortly after the Korean war had started, the US Army adopted a policy of allowing its soldiers to go on R&R (rest and recuperation) after six months of combat. The usual places for R&R were Kobe, Tokyo, and Hong Kong. I knew my choice would be Kobe, because it was the closest to Kure.

Our last words were:

"I pray to Buddha every day for your return. I have always love and always will love."

"I promise to return, and I will always love you."

After our goodbye, it was two days before we shipped out. During those two days of briefing, packing, and so forth, we weren't allowed to leave the base.

On the day of our departure, we rode the shuttle bus out the gate, through the village, and down to the dock. When passing through the village, I looked at our little home but didn't see her. Out of respect for my feelings, the gang never once picked at me on the way out. Even old Ben had nothing to say. The last time he had picked at me was two days before, when he was going through my duffle bag to see if I had hidden Namiko in it. I think they had learned to love her too.

> I have been here before,
> > But when or how I cannot tell:
> I know the grass beyond the door,
> > The sweet keen smell,
> The sighing sound, the lights around the shore.
> You have been mine before,—
> > How long ago I may not know:

But just when at that swallow's soar
    Your neck turned so,
Some veil did fall,—I knew it all of yore.

"Sudden Light"
Dante Gabriel Russetti (1828-1882)

The thing that hath been, it is that which shall be…and there is no new thing under the sun. Is there anything whereof it may be said, see, this is new? It hath been already of old time, which was before us.

Ecclesiastes 1:9 - Old Testament

Chapter II
Korea

We were transported from Japan to Korea aboard a three hundred foot seagoing vessel called a landing ship tank (LST). Because of its low speed, it was sometimes called "large stationary target." It was almost flat-bottomed, riding high in the water, and so designed for running up close on shore, opening its nose, unloading cargo and backing out of danger. In the Korean war, they were used mostly for transporting troops between Korea and Japan.

Since it was so hot and calm, we were allowed to sleep on deck. So that night, we spread our sleeping bags underneath stars so big and bright I had an urge to reach up and touch them. We lay there with a breeze carrying just enough spray to feel good, and talked of things young warriors have always talked of. What would our new assignment be? How many of us would stay together? What would combat be like? And on to our favorite subject, especially Ben's. What would the booze and babes be like? Would the Korean girls be anything like the Japanese?

Ben, Dexter, Ernst, Buck, and I were still together. Terry wasn't with us, because his brother had been killed, and he went home on an emergency leave. I never heard from him again. Wilson went back to his Air Force unit and I never heard from him either. When we arrived in Korea, Buck was assigned to a different unit than the rest of us. Later I heard he had been killed. Miraculously Ben, Dexter, Ernst, and I stayed together for all of my Far Eastern tour, bonding, and growing closer each day.

It is probably nearly impossible for non-military people to understand the bond and love between military buddies. It begins in basic training, which is designed for that. The drill sergeant's harassment drives you together. If one screws up, he takes it out on everyone. So, for self protection, you learn to look out for each other. You are driven to think and act as a team.

In the army, you sleep together, eat together, and shower together. You smoke, drink, chase women, dream, hate, laugh, and even cry together. You become so close you would die for each other, and some do. Brothers couldn't be closer, and here race has no place. Blacks and whites are true brothers-at-arms.

One often hears of the boys fighting for their country, or fighting for Old Glory, or fighting for some great cause. Country may be important to most, but the truth is, they are fighting for each other. That strong bond will not allow them to let their buddies down. The strength of this bond can be seen in the teary eyed World War II veterans speaking of their comrades of over fifty years ago.

Integrating the military with women and gays may work, but it is hard for me to see how the necessary bonding could take place. I love and respect women and have nothing against gays. In fact, some of my real heroes are women, and if a person wants to pursue a homosexual life, it's his or her business. Also, if anyone, regardless of sex or sexual orientation, is capable of doing a job, they should be considered for it. But not to the extent of disrupting an organization like the US military, and certainly not to satisfy some political agenda.

As to women, regardless of political correctness, they are different from men, and I am very glad they are. However, this difference does not make one sex overall superior to the other. A woman can do most things as well as a man, and she can do some things better. A man can do most things as well as a woman, and he can do some things better. So if a woman is capable of doing a job, she should have it; but the requirements shouldn't be lowered to fit the applicant. As to the military, there are many things to consider. Sex is certainly one of them. I wonder if anyone pushing the agenda of mixing men and women so closely together remembers being a horny young person when most thoughts are in some way colored with sex. If they do remember, and know anything about the military, it is hard to understand how they can honestly push such an agenda. It seems so unfair to put such temptation in front of healthy young people and then punish them for doing what comes naturally.

As to gays, I've had a few friends I knew to be gay, and probably a few that were that I didn't know to be. As I have said, I have nothing against any person pursuing the lifestyle they want to pursue, and they should be able to do so without harassment. But the thing most irritating to me in the gay rights movement is their attempt to convince themselves and everyone else that homosexuality is natural and normal. Nature provided people with either a penis or a vagina to keep the species going. That is biologically natural. That is the norm and any sexual activity other than between a male and female has to be in some way a biological or psychological error. If it is normal then 95 percent of the population is abnormal. How can that be? I wouldn't want to chance disrupting our military machine to satisfy less than 5 percent of the population.

Of course this question never came up when we were on this trip, because no one had ever dreamed of such a thing. But I can imagine my gang's reaction to such a question.

"What? Laying here on deck between a queer and a woman. Why that would be heaven to Ben," Ernst would have said.

"All I need is a woman, I already have the queer," answered Ben, pointing toward Ernst.

Anyway, with no women or declared gays, we made the trip and docked in Pusan Harbor about two hours before dark. It seems strange that the two most vivid memories of my Korean tour are the first and last day, but they are.

The first day upon docking, I came up on deck packed and ready to get off.

I overheard Dexter say, "Damn, what an ugly place."

Then Ben exclaimed, "What the hell is that smell?"

"The smell is human shit," said Buck, "they fertilize the fields with it."

My first thoughts and feelings are as clear as if it were yesterday. I looked up from the harbor at the ugly desolate hills surrounding it and at the dirtiest harbor I had ever seen. While my nostrils were being invaded by the terrible odor of the country, my thoughts were: *What am I doing here? Why did I volunteer for this?*

A young man often dreams of adventures to prove himself and has thoughts of bravado. But when faced with the real thing, it somehow begins to look different. I had often said and really believed I didn't care what happened to my body after the life left it. But upon seeing and smelling this place, my prayers were, "Oh Lord, please let me die some place else. If that can't be, please let my body be sent home." That was my first day.

Being young and flexible, it didn't take long to adjust to the new environment. That's the reason young men are drafted. They are not drafted because they are in better physical condition than a thirty year-old, because they are not. And they certainly are not as big and strong or nearly as smart; but they can adjust, relax, and rest when an older man can't.

Our living area wasn't bad. It was secured in the middle of the compound. The compound was about one square mile enclosed by an eight foot fence with barbed wire and sandbag bunkers. Here we had a Quonset hut covered with sandbags for barracks. We had a mess hall and a shower that sometimes had hot water. We also had toilets where you sat on a wooden board over a half barrel. The barrels, we called "honey pots," and the Korean farmers came around regularly to salvage the fertilizer from them. The "honey" was then placed around their fields in "honey" wells to be used as needed. That is what gave the country its famous aroma. The collection time seemed to always come at breakfast when stomachs are weakest, but after a few mornings of gagging and throwing up, I got used to it. A PX was on location where we could buy cigarettes, soap, and other necessities. And the Red

Cross (bless their hearts), a most noble organization, had hot coffee and doughnuts daily, which was a blessing on cold miserable days - a real morale booster. There was a place to get beer and liquor, but the only time the beer was cold was during cold weather. Then it would freeze and burst if not kept warm. For some reason liquor was hard to come by, except for scotch. It was plentiful and always crated in wood with straw. I think it came from the nearby British and Australians.

There was a barber shop with Korean barbers, and a movie hut. The movies must have been ones that my parents watched when they were youngsters. They were free, but nobody went if they could find anything else to do. One evening when we were too broke to go into a village, we were standing in line for a movie as Ben read the movie bulletin.

"*Northwest Passage*, hell, I done seen that," he said.

"No, Ben," said Dexter, "that was *Southwest Passage* we saw."

"Northwest-Southwest, same damn thing, horses just running in the other direction."

Those were our typical movies.

The whole compound was shared with the biggest wharf rats I hope never to see again. I was awakened several times by one crawling over my face. For years afterwards, I would dream of one jumping on my face and wake up screaming. They got so bad we declared war on them as well as the North Koreans. The compound even put out a bounty of one dollar per rat tail. It's a wonder we didn't shoot each other trying to eradicate them.

Another pest we had trouble with was head and body lice. I had never seen lice or crabs, but had heard many horror stories about how they would cover you in no time and how hard they were to get rid of. Then one day as I was putting deodorant under my arm, I saw one of the little varmints crawling. I immediately panicked and ran to the First Sergeant requesting to go on sick call.

"What's your problem?" He asked.

"I think I have crabs or lice."

He looked at me for a few minutes and then burst out in a big laugh.

"Here," he said, while handing me a small can of DDT powder. "Crabs and lice go with the duty over here. This won't keep you crab free, but it will keep them under control."

To my embarrassment, he was still laughing as I walked out with my little can of powder. From that day on, it was like my rifle, never far from hand. And I used it daily.

The day after our arrival, we were sitting around talking with the old heads, when Ben began inquiring about the available girls and booze.

"Man, there aren't any girls here," said one man.

"What do you mean no girls?" Asked Ben.

"Well there are a few down in the village, but that's off limits," said another.

"What do you do for girls?" Ben asked, beginning to sound desperate.

"Sometimes we sneak up on someone bending over in the shower."

"By all means don't drop your soap," replied another.

"Hmph," said Ben.

"Or did you see that street full of little horses outside the compound?" Asked another.

"Horses, I ain't gonna screw no damn horse," exclaimed Ben, "I ain't that low yet."

The conversation drifted away from girls and on to less important things. Then after thinking over the situation for a while, Ben interrupted the conversation with a question.

"How much does a horse cost?"

Ben didn't have to buy a horse though, because the village was full of girls, and most times, it wasn't off limits. It wasn't anything to compare to the glamorous bars and dolls of Japan, but the girls were pretty, and they had better liquor and colder beer than we could get on base. A carton of cigarettes and a bar of soap went a long way in the village. So we weren't so bad-off after all.

On any transfer, a soldier will lose some friends and pick up others. On this move, I lost Terry, Wilson, and Buck, and picked up Gainey, Snowden, and two more I had known in the states. One was Corporal James - now Sergeant James. I knew him in Camp Rucker, Alabama. He had already served a tour in Korea and had lost half his butt from shrapnel. He often said it was embarrassing to have been wounded in the ass. I liked him, and he, Dexter, and I had some good times together in Dothan, Enterprise, and Ozark, Alabama. The other was Sergeant First-Class Hill, now Master Sergeant Hill. Our relationship in the states had been anything but good. He had been my platoon sergeant in basic training and one night we had a real disagreement. This was in the final weeks of my sixteen weeks of basic training, and since the company needed boxers for their team, I had been excused from much of the routine in order to train and participate in the bouts. I think Hill resented this and one thing led to another until I challenged him to a fight in the gym. That was a big mistake. I found out then that my skills were nothing compared to his power as drill instructor backed by the US Army.

"Okay, shithead," he said, "I don't have to put on gloves to whip your ass. That's what these stripes are for."

And he was right. When the company commander got through drilling me out, and the mess sergeant had me for a week of eighteen hour days cleaning pots and pans, I had been whipped. I did tell him however, that one day we would meet when he was not protected by those stripes.

His only comment was, "Maybe, but I doubt it."

Time and events had erased him from mind. Then shortly after being in Korea, I was in the barber's chair for a haircut and shave. I had grown a long black handlebar mustache, and as I got up, I looked upon a tall slender blond man with a long blond handlebar mustache. He was staring intently at me as I was at him. Then we recognized each other at the same moment.

"Hey, Porter, how are you?" He said, reaching his hand out.

I remembered my threat, and I remembered his comment. But it didn't seem important anymore.

"How are you, Sergeant Hill?" I said, while sticking my hand out.

He and James became close in our group. They showed us around the area and taught us the important things, such as where the prettiest girls were, and the coldest beer, and how to get the most out of cigarettes, soap, and toothpaste. In other words, they taught us the necessary things for survival in a combat zone. They also knew how to handle lovesickness and broken hearts. For example, Snowden got a "Dear John" letter from his sweetheart and just lay around depressed. We kept trying to cheer him up, but nothing seemed to work.

Then Hill said, "Come on, John, let's go to the village. A trip to the whorehouse will clear your foggy head right up. Come on, I'm buying."

"You know my head has been a little foggy lately," said Ben. "Does that apply to me?"

"You were born foggy," said Dexter.

"Especially when it comes to women," added Ernst.

Hill must have known his medicine, because after a few treatments Snowden perked up and seemed to be as clear-headed as ever. Ben, of course, had to make regular trips to keep his clear.

We didn't have many American soldiers on base because a company of ROK (Republic of Korea) soldiers were assigned to us. I was assigned an area with one squad of American soldiers and two squads of ROKs. We also had ten Korean civilians to do any necessary work. I didn't get to really know any of the Korean soldiers, because they were rotated from place to place. The civilians I got to know pretty well, especially the ones who spoke English. One that I got to know well and felt close to was a Mr. Ha. He was an educated man and fluent in many languages, including English, Japanese, Chinese, Russian, and of course Korean. As a civilian he had been a teacher, but now worked for the U.S. Army. His main duty was to help with the language barrier and act as translator and interrogator of prisoners. He was about thirty years old and of small stature. He was very polite and helpful in any way he could be.

Another one special to me was Boy San, my houseboy. He was an orphan and only ten years old. I got him a pass so he could come on base. In fact, he lived most of the time on base, because he had nowhere else to go except the streets. Due to the war, the country was full of orphans with nowhere to go. There were some homes set up for them, but never enough, so most children Boy San's age or older were on their own. Some such homes were supported by personal donations from American soldiers. In fact I often visited one we helped to support, and it was a pitiful sight of filth, flies, sick children, and sometimes dead children. It was obvious from their appearance that many of the children had American fathers.

I paid Boy San well to keep my shoes shined and bunk made. The other soldiers used him also, so he was a well-off little fellow according to Korean standards. Besides paying him, I always gave him candy and spent a lot of time with him. He began thinking he belonged to me, and started calling me Papa San (meaning Papa or Father). The fellows encouraged that by calling him my boy, and saying I would have to take him home with me when I left Korea. None of us realized how seriously he was taking that idea until the time came for me to leave, and I began packing. To my amazement and everyone else's, he thought he was going with me. There he stood by my bunk smiling from ear to ear, with his few little belongings rolled into a bundle, laying beside my duffle bag. He was all ready to go to his new home, to the U.S.A., to the land of plenty, to a secure home away from his no home. I think then, when I looked down at his happy little anxious face, I saw the real him for the first time. There was a little boy, never in his memory having a home, but living in an orphanage until being put out to make room for some smaller child, then living in the street as best he could. He was ragged, cold, hungry, and miserable with no family or anyone to turn to. Then a savior in the form of an American G.I. came along and took him in, giving him a place to stay, with good food to eat and lots of other stuff. That G.I. was like a father to him. In fact it was the only father he had ever known, and all the other kind G.I.s were like family too. And best of all, he was now going to the United States with Papa San.

Oh my God, I thought as I looked down at him, *What a cruel, cruel joke. How could we have been so God damn ignorant? So ignorant and stupid not to see that he was taking the joke of going with me seriously*. How could I now tell him it was all a joke? A stupid dumb-ass joke! How could I now tell him that his Papa San, his security, was leaving him, never to return? Telling him he couldn't go with me was one of the hardest things I have ever done, and never in my life have I seen a little boy so broken-hearted.

He grabbed me around the waist sobbing and yelling, "No, no, Papa San, I go with you. Please, please."

The fellows had never seen me cry, but they did that day, and I wasn't alone. I got the gang's promise to look after him, but I didn't need it. I knew they would for as long as they could. Maybe he found a real Papa San. I always prayed that he did.

Carl L. Poston Jr.

Oh! What I would have given that day for Namiko's seashell of forgetfulness. Perhaps I did have it and didn't know. Perhaps we all have one, because if we didn't forget, we couldn't go on. Some experiences are just too painful to dwell on. So for self protection, they are pushed into the deep recesses of the mind, seldom coming to light. Even now, I try not to think about Boy San. In fact, it took two days to write about him, because of time out to cry.

Someone else who became special to me was not a person, but a dog of about sixty pounds. He was just a mutt with medium length tan hair. Where he came from, or how he got on base, no one knew. We only knew he was lucky to be there, because dogs didn't walk Korean streets for long. When caught, they were placed in a sack, and beaten tender to be cooked.

He had never known a world without explosions or gunfire. To him, it was just a part of the natural world, like strong wind or lightning and thunder. So, he paid it little attention. We named him G.I. Joe, and when not following me around, he made himself at home in our little office. There, he would lie by the oil heater, warm and well fed. G.I.'s could go in and out all day long, and he would never raise his head, but would only greet them with a lazy tail wag. But if a Korean opened the door, he was instantly up with ears pulled back and fangs flashing as a deep growl rolled from his throat. It had to be the difference in smell that brought him out of his peaceful sleep. The American smell meant food to him. The Korean smell meant he was to be the food. He was with us for about four months before mysteriously disappearing. We searched the base for him, but we never found out anything about him. I cussed all the Koreans in the area with every English and Korean word I could think of. I even flashed my M-1 around at them, saying, I would shoot any S.O.B. who had anything to do with his disappearance. If I ever had any friends among the Koreans, I probably lost them that day. After that, I got the feeling they avoided me whenever possible. I think they thought me to be a mad man, because some of them went to the company commander, telling him they were afraid I would shoot them.

Captain Cappell was our company commander. He was a husky bald-headed man from Pennsylvania and had been a college football star. He had earned his rank from Second Lieutenant to Captain while in Korea, and he was one of the best men and officers I have ever known. He more or less left the men alone if they did their duty. He wasn't spit and polish, but more like General and President Zachary Taylor - Ruff & Ready. He even allowed us to go out of uniform in rainy weather by wearing Jungle Jim hats and hip rubber boots, and many other non-regulation things. My estimation of him really went up one day when I witnessed him take a chewing out that should have been mine.

A colonel came through my area and took exception to something I hadn't done. I knew I should have done it, but I had failed to do so.

Looking at me, he barked, "Go find Captain Cappell and tell him to report here to me, and you come back with him."

"Yes, sir," I said, saluting and taking off.

We were back shortly, and the colonel lit in on him for what was my fault. I have never been more embarrassed for a man than I was for the captain that day. It hurt to watch that husky giant of a man stand there having to take the chewing out that runty little colonel put on him in front of me and everyone else present. It hurt even more because it was my fault. I had visions of the captain reaching over with his big hand, taking the runt by the neck, shaking him good and saying, "Shut the hell up." That, of course, didn't happen, and I waited for the colonel to leave, waited for what I had coming, knowing I deserved it.

After the runt left, the captain looked at me and said, "Porter, got a chew?"

He and I were two of a few in the company who chewed tobacco, and he often bummed a chew from me.

"Yes sir," I said, handing him the pack.

He took the chew and stood there looking the situation over, with hands shoved in his back pockets, in a very unmilitary manner. I stood beside him waiting and dreading my turn.

Then he said, "You do understand what the colonel said, don't you?"

"Yes sir, perfectly."

"Any questions?"

"No sir," I answered.

"Okay, see that it's done," and he walked away.

I watched his broad frame as he walked away, and thought, *that is a big man, big in more ways than physique. That is the kind of man I want to be, a man big enough to take that kind of ass cutting and not pass it on.*

That is the man the Koreans took their complaint to about me threatening to shoot them.

One morning after their complaint, the captain walked up to me and said, "Good morning, Porter."

"Good morning, sir."

"If you don't have anything pressing at the moment, I would like you to take a walk with me," he said.

"No sir, I don't."

"Good, then come along."

As we walked along he passed his tobacco to me, saying, "Have a chew."

"Thank you, sir."

"What is this I hear from our Koreans that they are afraid you will shoot them?"

"I did tell them that, sir."

"Did you mean it?" He asked.

"No, sir. I mean, I don't think so."

"You don't think so. You don't know?"

"Well at the time I was really mad. You do know about G.I. Joe, don't you, sir?" I asked.

"Yes, of course I know. I was rather fond of him myself, but that doesn't mean I can go around shooting or threatening to shoot the ones thought to be responsible for his disappearance. These people are our allies. They are part of the team. We have to work with them. I know it's disturbing about G.I. Joe, but you will just have to look at him like we do other missing G.I.s, a victim of war. Now do you understand there are to be no more such threats?"

"Yes, sir."

"Good, then go back to your business."

As I was walking away, he stopped me by calling my name.

"Porter."

"Yes, sir."

"There are times when I myself would like to shoot some of the sons-of-bitches."

"Yes, sir," I said and walked on.

Mr. Ha, always the diplomat, peace maker, and my friend, worked at bringing peace to our company. The whole time I knew him, he never addressed me by rank, and even though he was about ten years older than I, he always called me Mr. Porter.

"Mr. Porter," he said one day, "I am truly at a loss as to what happened to G.I. Joe. All the Koreans swear to me that they know nothing of his disappearance and I am inclined to believe them. I am speaking only of the civilian workers though and not the ROK soldiers. You know how they are rotated, so I really don't know about them."

"Most likely they are the bastards," I replied, "the damn dog eaters."

"I think so, unless he just wandered off," he answered.

"No he didn't wander off, he was too satisfied here," I said.

"I think you may be right, Mr. Porter."

After a long silence, he started up again. "Mr. Porter, I don't want to anger you. I know how you feel about the dog, and I am not trying to justify anyone abducting him. I know what a special dog he was to all of you G.I.s. Some Koreans, who can afford to, have special dogs too, but they are few in number. This is because we have a problem even feeding our hungry people, like Boy San, your houseboy and many other children." He looked at me to see how I was taking it and then went on.

"Again, I don't want to anger you."

"Go on," I said, "I won't be. Tell me what they say."

"Some wanted to know if Americans don't eat meat. Then Cheeker, who at one time worked in your mess hall, said that you had meat with every meal."

"Of course we do," I snapped, "but not dog."

"What kind of meat, Mr. Porter?"
"What kind of meat?" I asked.
"Yes."
"Well steak, bacon, chicken, fish," I said.
"Coming from cattle, pigs, fowl, and fish?" He asked.
"Yes. Animals raised to eat."
"Would it surprise you to know that the Koreans and Chinese raise dogs for that purpose? I also understand the American Indians ate dog meat."

I said nothing.

"Our Korean workers wanted to know if raising and eating dog meat is very different from raising other animals for food, such as cattle, pigs, and fowl."

As usual Mr. Ha had outmaneuvered me, so I sat there speechless and sullen. I could think of no argument to justify choosing one animal over another to be eaten. What is the criteria to determine who should be eaten and who shouldn't? Well, I thought, *dogs are just too friendly and faithful to be eaten*. But then, at one time, I had a pet rabbit and two pet chickens, and they followed me like a dog. They were friendly also. I had been around cows and there is nothing more friendly than a docile cow, like Bessie.

Maybe friendliness and faithfulness are not the right criteria. How about intelligence? A dog is very intelligent. But then, hadn't I read somewhere that a pig is more intelligent than a dog? Then a scary thought hit me. If intelligence is to be the criteria, would it be all right to eat retarded people, or people in a coma, or even young babies? We delight in eating babies of other species - namely veal.

Boy, did Mr. Ha know how to confuse a person who had already figured out everything about life.

He seemed to have a special knack for planting thoughts in my head to grow. This one would grow for the rest of my life. It would give me many wrestling matches with my conscience over meat eating and other abuses against animals, especially after the horrible factory farming came into existence. Following are the biggest causes of animal deaths per year in the US:

Fur	4.5 million
Animal shelters	5.4 million
Dissection	18 million
Research and testing	20 million
Hunting	200 million
Farm animals	9 billion

So it is obvious that the fork is the greatest killing instrument in the animal world – this includes humans, because more people die from obesity than from alcohol and cigarettes combined.

As I researched and saw more and more of the horrors that we humans inflict on other species, I became ashamed of being human. We are a species that can go to such great lengths to create all sorts of "feel-good" charities, such as The United Way, fight AIDS, feed the children, fight racism, and so on and so on. We wonderful humanitarians stand around such gatherings full of pride for what we are doing. We are there eating steaks, or fried chicken, or ham sandwiches with never a thought of the misery and horror our lunch went through before reaching our plate. We are a species claiming to be created in the image of God. I often wondered what that God looked like.

Maybe I shouldn't be so harsh and bitter towards people, because I really do believe that most people are good and kind at heart. I also believe that a truly mean and cruel person is hard to find, but I sometimes get so teed off at our arrogance, ignorance, and lack of empathy: arrogance for thinking that everything, including all other species were created only for our exploitation, ignorance of what our arrogance is doing to the environment and the misery it brings to God's other creatures, and lack of empathy because we can't get out of ourselves long enough to sympathize with other beings.

But who am I? Who am I to be critical of people when every breath I breathe and every step I take is paid for with lives of many other organisms? Without death, I wouldn't exist and neither could any other organism. Death and life depend on each other. They are one and the same. It is a vicious cycle which makes me a walking graveyard - a monument to death. Just think of the many different things that die for, and because of, my existence: cows, hogs, chickens, fish, rabbits, rats, insects, plants, etc. And why was I sent to Korea? Like Clint Eastwood in the movie *The Unforgiven*, you name it and I've killed it. So who am I?

Such questions have bothered me all my life, and still do. I have found no satisfaction in philosophy where Descartes discounts animals by saying they are only machines with no feelings. Kant saw ethics as a thing between men and didn't include other animals. I haven't found satisfaction in religion where for thousands of years, animals were sacrificed to feed a hungry god, and for a few hundred years, Catholics and Protestants burned people to appease their God. But at least credit can be given to Spain's Catholic priests for condemning the Incas' and Aztecs' human sacrifice and converting their heathen hearts. One way this was done was by throwing dogs and other animals into a hot oven and forcing the Indians to listen to the screams, so they could see what hell was like. Maybe those priests will have a special place in heaven for their work.

It seems to me we need a philosophy or school of ethics to not only include man to man, but man to man and all life. Albert Schweitzer suggested this, and if he had lived long enough, he may have come up with a philosophy to complete Descartes' and Kant's.

I know many things must die for me to live; but I feel a duty to make as little impact on life as possible. Out of necessity, I do kill ticks, fleas, flies, mosquitos, and so forth; but I seldom tear down a spider's web, and I relocate troublesome snakes. Seldom do I eat meat, because I don't have to. Besides, a vegetarian diet makes my body feel better as well as my conscience. I certainly can't speak for others, but these are personal decisions I can afford to make that make me feel good. The day may come when I have to kill to eat or kill in self defense. If it does come, I will do it, but I will do it with regret and apology.

I have often been asked the question, "How do you know plants don't feel pain?" My answer is, "There is no waste in nature. It gives nothing to organisms not needed. Pain is a very important sensation coming from the nervous system to protect the individual. So the purpose of pain is to cause the individual to move away from what is causing it. Plants don't have mobility to move or a nervous system, therefore, pain to them would serve no purpose."

At other times, I have been asked what good were my puny efforts of trying to curb animal abuse when almost six billion people throughout the world were in some way abusing animals. My answer is, I can only satisfy my conscience by doing what I can. Remember, the little things you do and say are like rain drops making a tiny brook, many brooks making a stream, many streams making one big river bursting all dams.

But we need to leave this subject, because I can easily get bogged down on man's inhumanity to other species. So let us go on with my story. However, Korea is not my intended story, so I will tell only enough to push it along and back to Japan.

Korea is a peninsula which abuts the Chinese province of Manchuria and the Russian province of Siberia, while Japan lies 110 miles across the Sea of Japan. The peninsula is only 500 to 600 miles long and varying from 90 to 200 miles wide. It is in no way a rich country, but for many years it has been fought over because of its location. It has long been the victim of a power struggle between Japan, Russia, and China.

At the end of World War II, the Russians sent 100,000 troops into North Korea to accept the Japanese surrender. Shortly afterwards, the Americans arrived in the south to accept the Japanese surrender there. Never was there any discussion of dividing the country into two occupation zones as Germany had been. But by the time the Americans arrived, Russia had essentially done that by setting up along the 38th parallel. They then set up a government in the north headed by Kim Il Sung and other Russian trained Communists. The U.S. in turn set up a government in the south headed by Syngman Rhee. In the United Nations, the Russians and Americans argued until 1948 over how to unite the country. Then the Russians quit talking and began pulling their troops out; but not before they had trained and equipped a large Korean army with the latest weapons, including tanks and aircraft.

In the south the U.S. had also pulled out their troops, except for a few advisers. However, they had equipped Syngman Rhee's army with only light weapons, and with no tanks or aircraft. The reasoning behind this was to keep Syngman Rhee from starting a war to unite the country.

In 1945, at war's end, the U.S. Army had over eight million men, but by 1950 it had been cut back to a little over one-half of one million, which were scattered around the world, mostly in Europe. The closest to Korea were MacArthur's occupation force of 83,000 in Japan. Most of those men were needed there.

That's the way things stood on early morning June 25,1950 when the North Koreans struck. By July 30, the South Korean Army and the few American advisers had been driven almost to Pusan, a port city on the tip of the peninsula. There, some miles from the city, a perimeter of defense was set up. In one month, the South Korean Army had been driven almost to the sea.

But by September when the U.S. and other United Nations members got together, the tide began to turn. Eventually this force consisted of fifteen nations: the United States, Great Britain, Australia, Canada, New Zealand, India, South Africa, France, Greece, the Netherlands, the Philippines, Thailand, Turkey, Belgium, and Sweden. Of course, the U.S. furnished the majority of troops and supplies.

Supplying this multinational force was a nightmare to the U.S. Army. Weapons and ammunition were pretty well standard, as well as clothing. However, Thailanders and Filipinos required smaller clothes. For food the Orientals had to have rice and fish. The Moslem Turks, of course, wouldn't eat pork. The Greeks didn't like some foods, such as potatoes. The good people back in the U.S. didn't want their young tender boys to be tempted with alcohol, but the British and French insisted on theirs.

But even with the many obstacles, by the last of October, the North Korean Army was defeated and pushed back across the 38th parallel, and almost into China. By all accounts, it seemed to have been a short conflict of about four months.

During June and July when the Communist army seemed sure to win and set the country up with a Communist government, Russia and China had little to say. But in August and September when it became evident that the north was going to lose, China kept warning that if any foreign troops crossed the 38th parallel, she would enter the conflict. MacArthur, who headed the UN Forces, ignored those warnings and sent the troops on to unite the country under Syngman Rhee's government.

As so often happens, our intelligence didn't have a clue as to the massing of Chinese Communist troops in the mountains of North Korea. These were not civilian soldiers, but experienced professionals, who had fought the Japanese and Nationalist troops of Chiang Kai-Shek for years. So without

The Japanese Princess and the American Rebel

knowing, our troops kept pushing until they were in the midst of 300,000 well-trained, hardened Chinese soldiers. In some cases, they were even surrounded by them. Then it became a war with China, and in December, the UN troops were in full retreat.

General Ridgway made this an orderly retreat by setting up lines of defense along the way. This retreat took place until the Communist momentum ran out. Then by June 1951, UN forces had set up a line of defense along the 38th parallel. This line held, and the war bogged down there with much action along it and many lives lost on both sides. The Communists, realizing they could make no further gains in war, agreed in July 1951 to begin talks on a truce. The talks went on for two years with many more thousands of deaths before a truce was signed in July 1953.

This Korea thing was called a conflict, a police action, and many other things, except war. Only Congress can declare war, and since Truman was well aware that the people had enough of war after 1945, he was reluctant to ask Congress for a declaration of war. Therefore, he went on proclaiming we are not at war. This was just a conflict. This was just a police action.

Let's look at some numbers of this police action versus our wars.

War	No. Years	Deaths
American Revolution	6	4435
War of 1812	3	2187
Mexican War	2	1733
American Civil War	4	618528
Spanish American War	1	361
World War I	4	52429
World War II	4	256330
Korea	3	33629
Viet Nam	9	57939

That is a very brief history of the Korean conflict and the reasons thousands of young Americans were there.

However, no history, brief or lengthy, tells the soldier's tale. A history can show the movement of armies, the strategy, the logistics, the generals, and so forth. It can show the big picture. But the soldier's part is so insignificant that if he didn't exist, the picture wouldn't change.

Neither can any romantic novel or movie tell the soldier's true tale. Romance is dashing and exciting and comes to a quick ending, so the victors can go back and celebrate to prepare for another engagement. Romance is an engagement between individuals. It is facing your opponent to a conclusion.

It is Greek warriors facing each other on the battlefield, or David facing Goliath. It is western gunfighters facing each other in a dusty street.

The modern soldier's tale is nothing like this. He seldom sees his enemy, but only mans his weapon to cover his line of fire or sends a shell miles away to kill. Likewise, a shell may fall on him from miles away. His is a tale of extremes: a tale of being hot or cold, or wet or thirsty, or bored from no action, or scared from too much action.

He is a victim waiting in a dirty stinking hole in the ground, waiting and praying that rotation comes before a shell does. Many come with nerve, but most leave with nerves.

Romance in war began dying in the butchery of the American Civil War, when weaponry outgrew strategy, and ended in the trenches of World War I.

My friend James' story comes as close as any to being the soldier's tale. He was in the first battle and back to see the war end. He was a Private First Class in the 24th Infantry Division in Kokura, Japan when the war began. As well as I can remember, this is his story in his words.

"Occupation duty in Japan was a ball. It was all light duty with nothing really to do. We even had houseboys and girls to do our housekeeping and to shine our shoes. Things were cheap and our money went far. Off base I even had an apartment with a car and a girlfriend. In fact that's where I was on the night of July 1. My platoon sergeant knew where I was and sent two MPs to get me.

"It was the middle of the night when the banging on the glass doors awakened me. It was pouring rain and I wondered, Who in the world could that be on such a miserable night. When I slid the door open, two MPs faced me.

"'We have orders to bring you back to base,'" they said.

"'Why?'" I asked.

"'I understand there is a little disturbance in Korea. Probably nothing serious.'

"I bid my girlfriend goodbye and told her I would see her in a few days.

"In our orientation, we were told a disturbance had occurred in Korea, and we were being sent over to police it. So we were equipped with weapons and a two day supply of C-rations and sent out into the rainy night to board waiting planes.

"At noon we landed on a Pusan airstrip. From there we were trucked up to Pyong Tack-Ansong to set up a defense. It was still raining. In a few days, the 34th Infantry arrived and took our place. This allowed our Colonel Smith to take 540 of us farther up where the road was bottle-necked between two hills. There we set up on both sides of the road to delay the Communist advance for as long as possible.

"It was then July 5th, five days since we had left Japan and the rain hadn't let up. In Japan and Korea it sometimes rains for weeks without letup. In those five days, we had learned that our little police action was to stop the well-trained and well-equipped North Korean Army.

"That morning we sat, or kneeled, or stood in wet muddy fox-holes. Some were knee deep in water. We ate our breakfast out of C-ration cans, sloppy with rain water, later trying to light wet cigarettes. Everything was wet, and moldy, and stinking. The whole country seemed to smell like a septic tank because the fields are fertilized with human waste.

"Except for a few officers and sergeants, we were a group of young men, half still teenagers, none really combat-trained. Just five days ago, we were living the soft easy life in Japan, with our movies, our beer, and our girlfriends, not even having to shine our shoes or make our beds.

"There I sat wet, scared, and miserable, wanting to throw up from the smell around me and the nervousness in the pit of my stomach. I sat there trembling and wondering how the U.S. Army expected 540 rookies to stop the thousands of Communists soon to be coming with their T-34 Russian tanks. We had no anti-tank mines to lay and only a few 105 mm howitzers with only a few armor-piercing shells. The other shells were just high-explosive, effective only on personnel.

"What really comes to the American soldier's rescue in such situations is his sense of humor. Some will always be cracking jokes. It must be some sort of defense thing to keep them from cracking up, the ever grumbling joking G.I.

'This is some damn police action.'

'I don't like playing cops and robbers.'

'Boy, when I get out of the army, I certainly don't want to be a cop.'

'I'll trade somebody a pair of dry socks for a dry cigarette.'

'If you chewed tobacco like me, you wouldn't have to worry about wet tobacco.'

'Hey, James, wonder who's lying in your dry bed at your apartment now?'

'Yea,' hollered another, 'and driving your Ford around.'

"And on and on.

"I didn't do much joking. I was too miserable. Then I became nauseated when I heard a creaking noise and looked down through the rain and saw three tanks rumbling toward us.

"As soon as they were within range, artillery fire was called in from the rear. The shells fell all about them, but they creaked on unaffected. When they got closer, we opened up with everything we had from both sides of the road. They rolled on. We just didn't have the weapons for it. We did manage, however, to kill many of the soldiers and hold them back until about noon. By then we had been forced to one side of the road and were flanked with rifle fire. We had lost contact with our artillery and had no air cover, so nothing was left to do but retreat. Colonel Smith tried to set up an orderly retreat, but it didn't work. Many of the men ran and left their weapons. Some even threw their rifles and helmets away, wanting nothing to interfere with their flight. It became more or less every man for himself. Even the dead and wounded had to be left behind with one soldier volunteering to stay with them. It is believed they were all executed.

"I stuck with Colonel Smith, and by nightfall about one hundred of us arrived safely at Ansong. For two days men kept drifting in individually or in small groups. One-hundred and fifty men never showed up. That was the first American battle of the war.

"Next we were sent to the city of Taejon to slow the advance while the Pusan perimeter strengthened. There we were issued the newly arrived 3.5 bazookas with shells that were supposed to be tank stoppers. After a few days we were routed from there in a disorderly retreat. That ended the 24th Division's holding action. Out of 12,000 men, over 3,600 were lost. General Dean was even captured and remained a prisoner. At least the Pusan defense perimeter was established and the Communist drive stopped there.

"My first experience in Korea was scared, wet, miserable, and hot. Some months later I was in North Korea's mountains at Koti-ri, still scared and miserable, but definitely not hot. The temperature stood around minus14 degrees. At that time, the U.S. forces were in full retreat from the Chinese armies, and in the confusion, I wound up there with 2,300 other soldiers, six or seven hundred surviving marines from dead Colonel Faith's unit, a thousand or more engineers, a few British marines and forty ROKs. We were completely surrounded by the Chinese, unable to make any move, so we set up a defense perimeter as best we could. There we waited. Waiting on what I didn't know, probably to freeze to death, I thought. Some did freeze to death, especially the wounded and weak ones.

"Then on December 7, General Smith with 12,000 marines fought their way to us. He refused to be evacuated by air, but said we were going out like marines and taking everything with us. He was as good as his word. The next morning at 3 A.M. in a blizzard, minus 14 degrees, six to eight inches of snow, we started out taking tanks, vehicles, big guns, prisoners, wounded, and dead. This was one time the dead didn't have to be prepared for purging by packing the nose, mouth, and rectum, and tying a tight string around the penis, because they were frozen like a block of ice. It was so cold nothing worked right, including guns and shells. Engines had to be run most of the time to keep from freezing. Everything froze: food, blood, medical supplies, and even feet and hands if not very careful. You dared not touch any metal bare handed or leave any skin exposed for long. It was so horribly cold and exhausting some would just lie down wanting to end it. But they weren't allowed to end it. They were forced to go on by others. Often we would run across fox holes with Communist soldiers frozen stiff.

"That's the way we came out of the mountains, while fighting all the way. As the front came out of the hills into Chinhung-Ni, the rear was still fighting. That is where a piece of shrapnel tore off part of my ass.

"After we were safely down out of the mountains, the wounded were flown to Japan for hospitalization. At last I was back in Japan from the little police action which was supposed to take a few days, and it was still a long way from over.

"I was in Japan for only a few days before being flown to a hospital in the states. After release from the hospital, I was assigned to Camp Rucker, Alabama. It wasn't long before I was bored with stateside duty, and here I am back again."

"What about your car and Japanese girlfriend?" someone asked.

"Fortunes of war, never saw or heard from either."

Now to see Korea and the war through South Korean eyes, I let Mr. Ha tell his story:

"Korea has not always been the backward country you see today. Few would know Korea had the first iron clad ships, with which she defeated Japan in the fifteenth century. They also fought the U.S. Marines in the nineteenth century until they withdrew. Furthermore, they had the printing press before Europe. Korea has a proud history, and I could go on and on; but I'll get to more recent times and my time.

"After the United States forced Japan to open up to world trade in 1853, the same pressure was put on Korea. We, however, held out until 1876 when Japan forced a treaty on us. The trade went well until Japan defeated Russia in 1905. Then they began to dominate Korea more and more. They even changed our name from "The Land of the Morning Calm" to "Chosen." Japan did make many improvements in the country, such as dams, roads, and railroads. But their harshness brought about much unrest and eventually guerilla warfare from the mountains. Those are the conditions under which I was born in 1922.

"As the years went by, things got worse, especially after Japan went to war with China. Then Japan really became a harsh overlord. So in 1938, my father slipped his family out of the country and into China, mainly so that my two younger brothers and I could get a better education. We lived in China until Japan surrendered in 1945. Then we returned to Seoul when I was twenty-three years old. Soon after returning, I obtained a teaching position. I had even brought a wife back with me who started teaching at the same college as I. Things were going well for us, in fact, for all of Korea. If only we had been allowed to remain one country and in freedom, I feel sure we would again have risen to pride and glory. But that was not to be, because the Communist north invaded the south and as you Americans would say, "All hell broke loose."

"After the invasion, I was in the middle of a class one day, when a South Korean Army officer with five soldiers burst into the room.

"'I hate to interrupt the class, professor,' he said, 'but I have a very urgent message for your students.' He then faced the students and addressed them.

"'Fellow Koreans, we haven't been able to stop the invaders from the north yet, and they are fast approaching our city. We need your help. So I have been instructed to press all young able bodied men into service to defend your city and country.'

"He then began walking among the desks, asking each student his name and age. Anyone over 15, he entered his name in a little book and motioned for his soldiers to escort him out of the room. My youngest brother, 18 years old, was taken with them. Probably none of these young men had ever fired a weapon, much less had any military training. My brother and I never had any. So I voiced a protest by asking the officer who had authorized him to do this. He turned and looked me over for what seemed like a long time, and then walked up close.

"'How old are you, professor?'

"'Twenty-eight.'

"'Take him,' he said to the soldiers.

"So I, my brother, and nearly my whole class wound up in the ROK army defending the city of Seoul against the Communists.

"When it became obvious the city could not be defended, refugees flooded the roads trying to leave, later to be followed by army stragglers. I was never able to contact my wife or father, but I prayed they were among the first to leave. I was especially concerned for my wife, because she was five months pregnant.

"A few days later, on June 28, the city fell, and I became a prisoner of war, along with thousands of others, but not for long. About fifty or sixty of us were placed in a room so tightly packed that we all couldn't sit at the same time. The doors were locked and guards placed at the doors and windows. There we stayed with no food or water for a day and night. We did, however, get organized enough to use two corners of the room for a toilet.

"After the day and night, the door was opened and all officers and non-commissioned officers were called out, and the door closed.

"'They are going to feed the officers first,' I said to a man next to me. 'We will be next.'

"It wasn't long before they were back for us. They led us out three at a time and tied our hands behind our backs.

"*How are we suppose to eat like this?* I thought.

"Then they marched us outside and lined us up in military columns, facing some men kneeling before us. I counted thirteen of them and recognized some as being the officers taken from our room.

"Behind the kneeling prisoners stood two Communist soldiers with pistols in hand, one behind each outside prisoner. An officer stood between them and a little to the rear. On a sharp command from the officer, each soldier fired a bullet into the brain of the kneeling prisoner in front of him. Then they stepped smartly behind the next one doing the same, and on down the line. When they met in the middle on the thirteenth, he being the odd man, got the privilege of receiving two bullets, one from each executioner.

"While standing and watching, and knowing we were next, I was sending up a silent prayer. I am sure everyone else was doing the same, although many were not quite so silent. Nerves got the better of one, and he took off running with hands tied behind his back. Like frightened animals following the first to flee, three or four more took off after him. Almost instantly all of them were cut down by gunfire. Another man close to me fainted, but that didn't save him, because a soldier stepped up and fired two bullets into his prone body.

"After all the gunfire, the officer addressed us in a harsh voice.

"'We are here to liberate our people and unite our country. You can be a part of this. In other words, you can join us or join the traitors lying before you.'

"No one chose to join the traitors, so we were separated and placed individually in different units of the Communist army. That way we could be watched closer and therefore controlled better. Just a few days ago, I had been fighting for South Korea, now I was fighting for the North Korean Communists.

"So I went with the Red army fighting its way down to what would later be called the Pusan perimeter. I may have even faced some of you there.

"I know many people wonder why I didn't escape. Believe me, I looked for an opportunity to do so, but it never came. I was watched so closely, and several times I witnessed several men shot for foolishly trying to escape. I was more than anxious to get away from the atrocities I saw. I saw many prisoners taken, but none were kept as prisoners. They were either forced into the Communist army as I had been or executed. On the retreat north I even witnessed American prisoners shot.

"During the Communist retreat north, I found myself back in Seoul defending the city for the second time; but now defending it for the Communists, instead of against them. The city fell and I saw the opportunity to escape by surrendering to the Americans. I was then a prisoner of war for the second time. How ironic, to have defended the city twice and be captured twice, once by each army.

"By 1952, the UN forces had captured approximately 176,000 enemy soldiers. The Red Cross determined 38,000 of these soldiers to be South Koreans pressured at gun point into the North Korean Army as I had been. They were released. I was captured in 1950, but even before 1952 smaller numbers had been released the same way. However, I was not among the lucky ones. I was among the ones who no one listened to and were sent off to prison camps. I was sent to the Koje Island Prison Camp. Koje is a rock barren island five miles off the mainland, not far from Pusan. It is about twenty miles long and nine miles wide. Eventually it held 150,000 Korean and Chinese prisoners.

"The island had been picked for a prison camp for two reasons. One reason was economics. Since it was surrounded by water, the prisoners couldn't walk away and there were few able to escape by water. It needed only a small American force for guards, therefore freeing more forces for line duty. The other reason was to help extinguish the fires of Communist propaganda concerning prisoner abuse. Here the prisoners were left to police themselves.

"That's the way Koje was run. Once on the island, a prisoner became a citizen of the prison camp, subject to its law and no other. He was lost to the world and forgotten. There was no head count, or bed count, or any other kind of count. In fact the guards dared not enter the compound for any reason. Often the prisoners taunted the guards by daring them to come inside the compound. The prisoners had no fear because they knew the guards were under strict orders to shoot only in self-defense. This policy was implemented because of Communist propaganda of prisoner abuse. On a few occasions, the prisoners even tortured and killed anti-Communist prisoners while guards helplessly looked on.

"The day I entered through that gate of hell, I and the other new prisoners were escorted by other prisoners to an area where we were interrogated and assigned to quarters. I soon learned the camp was organized and firmly governed by the Communists. Inside were a general, a colonel, and numerous planted spies who had organized the camp into military units. They even had connecting tunnels dug throughout a large area and stockpiled with hand made weapons. Messages with the outside Communists came and went on a regular basis. Plans were eventually laid for a break out with outside help. And to show how bold and in control they felt, a Communist flag flapped in the ocean breeze, high over the compound.

"That was a government that truly ruled by terror, because anyone showing any sign of being anti-Communist was brought before court and tried. If found guilty they were executed on the spot. In all the trials I witnessed, no one was ever found innocent. I even saw six people tried together and executed together.

"That is where I and many more South Koreans were placed. We were men who had been forced into the Communist army at gunpoint. We dared not speak out in any way, much less claim we were there by mistake and wanted out. All my hopes of being freed died. I no longer thought about it. My only thoughts were on staying alive.

The Japanese Princess and the American Rebel

"In 1952, I witnessed the foolish American General Dodd, commandant of the post, lured into the compound and taken hostage. He was humiliated, abused, and forced to sign a propaganda statement of how the prisoners were being abused on the island.

"Shortly after that embarrassing incident, my prayers were answered when General Hayden Boatner brought tanks and troops to break up the organization. He separated all the prisoners into smaller groups. Then after two years of hell, I was able to speak to someone, and it wasn't long before I was identified and set free.

"During that time both of my brothers were killed. One with the Communist army, the other with the South Korean Army. My father was killed when the Communists shelled Seoul. I have never found out what happened to my pregnant wife. For a long time I searched for her, and prayed that she would show up somewhere. But now I know she won't. And now I am here working with the U.S. Army, my third army, and I pray never to be another prisoner of war."

That is a view of the Korean war through the eyes of the American soldier and the South Korean citizen. Now we return to the story of my Japanese Princess.

Even though Namiko couldn't read and write English, and I couldn't read and write Japanese, we corresponded almost daily. This was arranged by her writing in Japanese and Aunt Mitchie rewriting it in English to be mailed to me. In turn, I would write in English and Aunt Mitchie would either read or rewrite it in Japanese for Namiko. This was a good arrangement which worked well except for the daily burden on Aunt Mitchie. Also, I wasn't at ease in expressing some things I knew Aunt Mitchie would read. I thought Namiko must feel the same way, because her letters seemed a little formal and not really like her. Then it dawned on me that Mr. Ha may be able to do this for us. I approached him about it, and he was delighted.

So my next letter was in Japanese. I told her of Mr. Ha, and that from then on she could write to me in Japanese. I immediately saw a big difference in her letters. We were then able to freely express our feelings and love and to mention the endearing little things so important to lovers. It would seem distance and time should have cooled our love, but it didn't. It didn't in my case anyway, and from her letters, she must have felt the same way. It seemed that our love, like a healthy slow growing vine, just grew and grew.

One day I got a real surprise after opening a letter from her. It was headed in English as follows:

My Dearest Beautiful Big American Rebel,
I have been learning English. I wanted to surprise you. I love you very much.

The rest of the letter was in Japanese. She said Aunt Mitchie was teaching her English, and teased by saying, "I have also been painting a lot now that I don't have you to disturb me so, but I would gladly give up all painting just to have you disturb me a little."

That vividly brought to mind the trips we used to make to her favorite waterfall where she often went to paint. It was a beautiful spot where a brook spilled its water over a ledge making a lovely little waterfall. After its fall the water rushed along, splashing and gurgling over the rocks, in such a hurry to join the big water of the bay. It was one of the most secluded spots on the island and only reached by foot. It was a very quiet and peaceful place. Quiet, that is, except for the brook and waterfall, and that was a most peaceful and relaxing sound. It was a perfect place for painting, or picnicking, or just sitting.

On such trips, she would prepare a light lunch and with the lunch, a blanket, and paint paraphernalia, up the trail we would go for a perfect day. Once there, we would spread the blanket, and she would be seated with a fold-up easel in front and paint and brushes beside her.

As she painted, I sat to the side painting also. My intention was to capture the very essence of beauty by painting her at work in that setting. I tried to show a bright clear day with a few clouds drifting high overhead beneath a deep blue sky. Our position was high enough and not too far from the bay, so we felt a good breeze. I also wanted to capture the breeze in the twisted and rugged little trees (probably ancient ones), by showing the branches gently waving all about. When the breeze grew tired of teasing the trees, it would switch to the waterfall and send a light spray our way. From this spray, droplets of water clung to the nearby grass blades and spider webs, which glittered like diamonds in the sun. I also knew I had to show the water rolling over the ledge into the rocky little stream—the water which never slowed after its fall, but just hurried on its way, splashing and gurgling.

It seemed to be in such a hurry that I wanted to yell at it and say, "Hey, water, where are you going in such a hurry?"

But I didn't have to ask, because I knew. It was rushing down to the bay to join the ocean waters, there to be picked up by the sun and dropped as rain somewhere else in the world, perhaps to be dropped in another little brook like this, or in time, back to this same little brook. But it still seemed senseless to be in such a hurry. The ocean wasn't about to dry up.

I wanted to add, "Slow down a bit, water. There is no need to rush so. There is no end to your job, you know. It is a circle. But you are really no different than I. We all run in our circles seeking our source."

"The dew drop slips into the shining sea."

Capturing the scenery wasn't the hard part. The hard part was to capture the beauty of that little goddess leaning over her canvas hard at work. How could I capture the shine of the long black hair hanging down her back? How was I to capture her perfect figure, sitting with legs crossed in the yoga position? How was I to show the enchanting way she had of swinging her head and tossing the hair over her shoulder? The way she turned from time to time, rewarding me with a smile to assure me I wasn't being neglected, was almost beyond capture.

All those things I wanted to capture in my painting, and I did, and much more. It turned out to be an excellent picture, and even today, after over forty years, it hasn't faded one bit. However, I have been selfish with it, because I have never shown it to anyone. It's not that I'm ashamed of it, but I just didn't know how to show it. You see, it is painted in my mind.

Sometimes when sitting on the blanket watching her paint, I would be overcome with temptation. Then I would ease up behind her, put my arms around her waist, and begin kissing her ear and one side of her neck.

One time, I did this, and with her concentration broken, she said, "Stop. You make me mess up."

"Okay," I replied, while going to the other ear.

She turned her head toward me, saying, "That not stopping."

"I will," I said, and then proceeded to kiss each eye, her nose and then lips.

She dropped her paintbrush, put her arms around my neck, and began to passionately return the kiss.

Abruptly, I broke free and said, "Okay, now I stop. Go back to your painting," and I lay back on the blanket.

"Oh no, too late now," she exclaimed. "I already mess up."

Then falling on me, she began kissing me the same way I had kissed her.

"Stop," I said, "go back to your painting."

"Okay," she said between kisses.

"When?" I asked.

"Soon."

Being smothered in kisses, I could say no more.

Then she suddenly stopped the kisses, sat up, and said, "Now I paint."

"Oh no you don't," I yelled, while pulling her back down, "Too late now, you have really messed up."

We lay there tussling, and laughing, and kissing, and not aware of much else except each other. We were certainly not aware of painting, or the army, or Korea. The world just faded away except for a vague awareness of the cool breeze, light spray, and the brook's happy song. In those moments, her Buddhist point of view that nothing is separate but everything is interconnected seemed so obvious. That wonderful togetherness, that wonderful oneness with the breeze, the spray, the sun, the brook, and her. I would never be free of her, nor did I want to be.

It seemed that every one of her letters had more and more English words and phrases, and before long she wrote many complete sentences. I was amazed at how fast she was progressing in the language. Mr. Ha even remarked on how well she was improving. He often gave her hints on the language, and sometimes a part of her letter would be to him answering some question he had asked her about Japan or her art. He eventually spoke about her as if he knew her. He did know more intimate things about us than anyone else did. Sometimes I felt myself getting a little annoyed or jealous that he became so familiar with her.

But when not thinking with my heart, I was sure he had no other motive than curiosity. He was a very educated man and full of curiosity about everything. We talked for a long time on questions he asked about the U.S., my state, racism, U.S. lifestyle, and so forth. He knew a lot about the Far East, but his education had been limited concerning the U.S., so he got as much as he could out of us Americans. He was a most interesting man, and I enjoyed him very much; but being not much more than a boy, my education and background were limited, so I couldn't appreciate him then like I could now. I would give anything for the opportunity to talk with him now.

In fact, he told me things about Namiko I had never noticed. For example, from her writing (which he called brush strokes), he mentioned she was skilled in calligraphy. According to him calligraphy became an art form in China long ago. Later, the Koreans used Chinese characters in the artistic brush strokes. Then it went to Japan where it is now popular in Buddhist works.

"Since she is so active in Buddhism, that is probably where she began learning it," he said. "Hand me one of her letters and I will show you. Of course her letters aren't calligraphy, but from them I can see that she is a calligrapher. See here," he said, pointing to the letter, "notice how the characters flow together in such balance and beauty."

I saw then for the first time the painstaking beauty of her letters or characters.

"You have a very talented young lady," he said.

That, I already knew.

"In our next letter," he said, "let's ask her to write some Buddhist text in calligraphy and send us, and I will show you."

I didn't miss that "our next letter," but I agreed.

It was in the fourth letter after our request as follows:

The Japanese Princess and the American Rebel

This is Mr. Ha's translation of it.

> The colorful flowers are fragrant, but they
> must fall. Who in this world can live forever?
> Today cross over the deep mountains of
> life's illusions and there will be no more
> shallow dreaming, no more drunkenness.

One day at mail call I was surprised with a package from Namiko. In the package was a letter and two books. The books were *The Book of Tea* and *Bhagavadgita*. They were both English translations. In the letter Namiko said Aunt Mitchie had found these English translations and thought I would enjoy them since I had previously shown much interest in the subject. I thought back to the day I was introduced to them in Japan.

One evening when returning to Mitchie's home after a visit to the Zen Buddhist Temple and a tea room, I asked what the significance of tea was to Japan. Why was it so important, and what exactly was the tea ceremony? Does it have a religious significance, or is it secular?

It always excited Namiko when I asked any questions about her country or her people. She seemed pleased that I was interested and always did her best to answer. However, if Mitchie was present, she always allowed her to give the involved answers because of her fluent English. Often on such questions, they would converse with each other in Japanese, and then Mitchie would translate to me. Mitchie seemed to enjoy educating me as much as Namiko did. However, it wasn't a one-sided affair, because they were always questioning me about the United States. I could enlighten Namiko on some things because she had never been out of Japan, but Mitchie gave me much more than I could return. Besides her having lived in the United States, she was far ahead of me in years and education. She, however, had never traveled in the southern part of the U.S. and had questions about my state. But let's go back to my question about tea.

"No," Mitchie said, "It is not a religious ceremony, not anymore anyway. Tea has been important to Japan for many, many years. The plant is native to southern China and was cultivated thousands of years ago as a delightful drink and as a medicine. It was ingested for medical uses and also used as a paste for rheumatism. Now, as you know, it is enjoyed as a drink all over the world, especially in England. But nowhere has it reached the importance it has in China and Japan. In religious ceremonies, it did become important to the Taoists of China, but I don't think it was ever a religious thing to the Buddhists. However, since Zen Buddhism is heavily influenced by Taoism, the Zen monks of Japan used it to help stay awake during their long hours of meditation. So through Zen the tea ceremony developed in Japan.

"Our tea ceremony or Teaism comes from Zenism which comes from Taoism. It's main contribution now is not to religion but to art. However, to me, it seems awful hard to separate religion from art."

I thought of John Ruskin writing, "art consists of one soul talking to another."

Namiko then interrupted Mitchie in Japanese.

Mitchie listened to her, and then turned to me saying, "Namiko has reminded me of a book I have in which certain passages should explain this matter far better than we can. However, it is written in Japanese so I will have to read it to you." She got the book and sat back down.

"This is *The Book of Tea*," she said, "and was written in 1906 by Kakuzo Okakura. Most of the books were printed in English because Okakura wanted to explain the art and culture of Japan to the western world. This copy is one of the few Japanese prints. I wish I had an English copy for you, but I don't even know where to find one. But since most copies are in English you should be able to find one, and if you do, you should get it, because it really explains Japanese art and culture in relation to Teaism. This passage I am going to read is from page twenty-one of what Taoism is.

> The Tao literally means a path…
> Lao Tzu himself spoke of it thus:
> 'There is a thing which is all containing,
> which was born before the existence
> of Heaven and Earth. How silent!
>
> How solitary! It stands alone and
> changes not. It revolves without
> danger to itself and is the mother
> of the Universe. I do not know
> it's name and so I call it the path…'"

After reading the passage, Namiko began speaking in Japanese and Mitchie translated.

"By following this path one can experience the bliss and happiness and peace of Zen. It is a path, however, that one has to travel alone. It is like Christian salvation in that it is a personal experience. Even though it has to be traveled alone, sometimes others can help lead one to the beginning of the path. There are numerous ways of finding this path, but for Zen Buddhist, Zanzen meditation is most often used and said to be the best. Beauty in art communicates something of this path, and that is where the tea ceremony comes in, along with flower arranging and painting. And especially Namiko's painting," added Mitchie while looking over at her with a proud smile.

"Now I read from page seventeen to show how the tea ceremony holds the ideas of Taoism and Zenism," Mitchie continued.

> "The tea room was an oasis in the dreary waste of existence where weary travelers could meet to drink from the common spring of art - appreciation. The ceremony was an improvised drama whose plot was woven about the tea, the flowers, and the paintings. Not a colour to disturb the tone of the room, not a sound to mar the rhythm of things, not a gesture to obtrude on the harmony, not a word to break the unity of the surroundings, all movements to be performed simply and naturally, - such were the aims of the tea - ceremony. And strangely enough it was often successful. A subtle philosophy lay behind it all. Teaism was Taoism in disguise."

Then she closed the little book and said, "think back now on the tea room we were in today. Remember how plain, bare and simple everything was, no clutter, no distractions, everything arranged to rest your mind, everything as natural as possible. Even the little trees over the walkway are shaken regularly to allow the leaves to fall and lay naturally. When they become old and mashed, they are removed and new ones shaken down. That is Zen: simple, peaceful, and natural. It is said not, but it is hard for me to see it as not religious."

"I agree," I said, really impressed with the story.

I couldn't believe they were thoughtful enough to find an English version of the two books and send them to me. How I did love those two women.

I was just as proud of the *Bhagavadgita* ("Lord's Song") as I was *The Book of Tea*. It is the most important religious text of Hinduism and was written in about the year AD 100. In thumbing through it and looking over the different passages, I could almost hear Mitchie reading from it. I think I could have listened to her all day. I found it to be just as interesting as the Bible. Here are a few of the passages that so entranced me:

> "That which is can never cease to be;
> that which is not will not exist.
> Thou grievest where no grief should be!
> Thou speak'st
> words lacking wisdom! For the wise in heart
> mourn not for those that live nor those that die.
> Nor I, nor thou, nor anyone of these
> ever was not, nor ever will not be,
> forever and forever afterwards.
> All, that doth live, lives always!
> To man's frame as there came infancy
> and youth and age,
> so come these raisings up and laying
> down of other and of other life-abodes…"

I had another big surprise when I showed the books to Mr. Ha. He was as excited as a child at Christmas. He had, of course, known of both books but had never had the opportunity to read them. So we took turns with them.

Then Mr. Ha's birthday arrived, and I gave him both books as a present. I thought he had been excited when I received them, but that was nothing compared to his excitement when I gave them to him. To my embarrassment, he hugged and hugged me in front of everyone. I even began to fear that he was going to kiss me.

As I said, this is a love story and not a war story, but there are two more short stories I wish to tell before going back to the story of Japan.

One is an experience that none of us are likely to forget, especially Ben Carr. Everything turned out all right, but it could have been a real tragedy. It took place on the south side of our compound, which we called South Fence.

The American soldiers didn't walk guard duty around the compound because we had ROK soldiers for that. The Americans only acted as sergeant and officer of the guard to check on the Koreans, making sure they walked their posts in a military manner. But on this particular day, Ben was walking guard duty as punishment for one of his screw-ups. Besides having guard duty, he had

The Japanese Princess and the American Rebel

been restricted to the compound for a week. Not being able to visit the girls in the village made for a long week, and it was beginning to take its toll on him. So he walked along the eight-foot fence with a rifle on his shoulder daydreaming about the booze and girls in the village. Suddenly his dream became very real when he saw a pretty girl approach the fence, looking at him and smiling.

"Hey G.I., got a cigarette?" She asked.

"Yeah," Ben replied, handing her one through the fence and lighting it for her.

"What are you doing here?" He asked. "You know this fence is off limits."

"I see you, think maybe you lonesome, want company," she said.

"Yeah, well this fence is off limits to you, and besides how much company can you be with this fence between us?"

"Maybe lot," she said while reaching through the fence fumbling with his fly.

"You better leave before the sergeant of the guard comes."

He kept telling her to leave, but he wasn't backing up from the fence, and in no time her experienced hands had his fly open.

"For ten dollar I show what company I can be," she said.

Ernst always said Ben's brain was in his pecker and now the girl had his brain in her hand, and he was completely under her control.

"I don't have ten dollars," Ben said weakly, "I only got five."

"That do," she said.

He laid his rifle down, took the five out and handed it to her.

"Okay," she said while taking the five, kneeling and going about her business of earning it through the fence.

Ben couldn't seem to get close enough to the fence. He was now holding on to it with both hands glorying in his good fortune. Things couldn't be better. He even had girls coming up to the fence for him. He might even arrange to have her come regularly and maybe bring whiskey. He could hardly wait to tell the gang of his good fortune. He was standing there basking in his glory when suddenly he felt her teeth clamp down too tight for comfort.

"Ouch! Not so damn hard, that hurts," he yelled.

At the same time a Korean man suddenly appeared. Startled, Ben tried to pull back, but he couldn't move because the girl's teeth had a bull dog grip on him.

The Korean man speaking excellent English, said, "Stand firm, give me your money and cigarettes, or she will bite it off."

By then Ben's legs were so weak he could hardly stand, much less stand firm.

"I don't have any more money," Ben pleaded.

"Give me your wallet," the man insisted.

The girl's teeth tightened.

"Ouch, you bitch, you bastard," Ben yelled as he handed his cigarettes and wallet through the fence.

It so happened that Dexter was sergeant of the guard that day and he walked up on them unobserved. He couldn't see the man because Ben and the girl were blocking him from view. What he saw was the girl on her knees and Ben pressed up close to the fence clutching it tightly with both hands and groaning as if in ecstasy. But sometimes it's hard to tell the difference in the sounds of ecstasy and agony.

Dexter burst out laughing saying, "Damn, Ben, you can't wait until you get off duty for your fun?"

"Fun, hell, the bastards are robbing me. Shoot'em," yelled Ben!

The Korean man looked at Dexter alarmed, but calmly said, "Put your rifle down or your friend will be minus a part of him."

The girl tightened her grip and Ben yelled. "For God's sake do what he says, Dexter."

Dexter began easing his rifle down when the Korean man said, "No, pick up his rifle and place both over by that post," which was about fifty feet away.

Dexter looked at him and then at Ben, reluctant to part with his weapon, not knowing that they didn't have one.

"Do it, Dexter, do it and hurry," pleaded Ben.

Dexter complied and returned.

The man then said, "give me your wallet."

"You are crazy as hell if you think I'm giving you my wallet."

The girl tightened and Ben yelled, "Give it to him. I'll pay you back double, ten times."

Reluctantly, Dexter handed it through the fence. The man took it, the girl turned loose, Ben fell back on the ground groaning, and Dexter ran for his rifle. But by the time he had his rifle, the man and girl had disappeared with both wallets.

Dexter looked down at Ben laying on his back, rolling from side to side and groaning.

He was saying over and over, "My God, I'm ruined," while holding both hands over his manhood as if to guard it from further harm.

Dexter started to go for help but then thought he might better check Ben first, because he may be bleeding so bad first aid may be required.

"Move your hands, Ben, let's have a look," demanded Dexter.

Ben slowly opened his hands as if he were holding a bird that might fly away. Both were afraid of what they would find. Ben couldn't stand to look so he kept his eyes tightly closed while Dexter looked to see how serious the damage was. He lay there groaning, waiting for the bad news, when Dexter burst out in a big laugh.

"There is nothing wrong with it, except some tooth marks," said Dexter between peals of laughter.

The Japanese Princess and the American Rebel

Ben opened his eyes wide and sat up examining it over and over, almost in tears from relief knowing he wasn't ruined for life, but in no time his relief started turning into acute embarrassment.

He hollered at Dexter, "There ain't a damn thing funny, I could have been ruined."

"Well ruined or not, you better put it back in your pants and get back on guard duty. By the way, how do you suggest I write this in my report?"

"Report! You don't have to mention it. Nobody knows but us. Nobody else needs to know."

Ben knew Dexter wouldn't make an official report of it, but was trying to convince him not to tell the gang about it.

"Very well," said Dexter, "I won't write it up."

"Good."

As Dexter walked off, he looked back and said, "But just wait until the gang hears."

"Wait a minute! Come on, buddy, you don't have to tell them either," pleaded Ben, now following along behind him.

"And I want my twenty bucks back that was in my wallet," said Dexter.

"I'll give it back. You know I will."

But that story was too good for Dexter to keep to himself. He had to let us know. In fact, it was too good for us to keep within the gang, and before long the whole compound knew. Poor Ben was a long time in living that down. Following are some of the things he had to endure.

"Hey Ben," I said, "you may be able to get a purple heart from that."

"If he gets a purple heart, I should get a medal for saving his sorry pecker," said Dexter. "And besides, he only paid five dollars while I paid twenty to save it."

Ernst came in with his German accent, "Dexter, you should have let her bite it off and done him a favor. That would have eliminated all his problems."

"I wouldn't try for a purple heart, if I were you, Ben," said James. "The army may decide to court martial you for carelessly endangering government property."

"All of you kiss this ass," yelled Ben.

That was our most enjoyable war experience. It also cut down on the boredom, because any time anyone wanted a fight all he had to do was say to Ben:

"Had any good blow jobs lately?"

The other story is the story of a battle that came as a surprise. Our company began organizing a boxing team to compete in some upcoming events. Our team leader and trainer was Jim Brown (No, not the singer). As far as I know, this James Brown couldn't sing, but he sure could fight. He was a black man about twenty-five years old and fought light-heavy even though he was only five feet seven inches tall. His short stature was a big disadvantage to him as a light-heavy, but he made up for it in other ways. He had huge arms on enormous shoulders and a little head about the size of a grapefruit. Like a turtle he would pull that little head between those huge shoulders, leaving little target for his opponent. That is how he got the nickname of Turtle Brown. When up close, few opponents could stand under his powerful body blows and uppercuts. He also had the reputation of being a good trainer and knowledgeable about boxing, so he was put in charge of organizing and training the team.

Our gym was a clear spot outdoors between two Quonset huts, which was as good as any other team had. A few days after our training had started, Turtle called us to a huddle.

"Gather around, fellows and I will give you a line up as to who is to fight who."

He went down his list, having a match for everyone except me.

"What about me?" I asked.

"Last but not less, you are the lucky one," he replied.

"Well, tell me about my luck."

"Okay, the Koreans wanted a part in the bouts to show us Americans up, so they entered the name of one of their heroes."

"And he happened to be my weight?"

"No, in fact, he is thirteen pounds lighter than your 148 pounds, but you are the closest we have, so you are it."

"Is this guy any good?"

"Your guess is as good as mine. I understand that at one time he was some district champion. That's about all I know of him."

"He is not a professional, I hope."

"I don't think they have a clear line of separation between amateur and professional," he answered.

"Boy, it gets better all the time. I now see why you say I'm the lucky one. Any of you fellows want to take my lucky place?"

Turtle continued, "There is a decision we have to make now. You need to decide whether you want to wear shoes or not."

"Wear shoes! Why shouldn't I wear shoes?"

"Because if you wear shoes, you can't kick."

"Why should I want to kick?"

"Oh, I forgot to mention that he will be barefooted because he is a kickboxer."

"A what?"

"Yes, a kickboxer," he affirmed.

"But I'm not a kickboxer."

"I know," replied Turtle with a laugh, "but it's no big deal. I have a plan."

"Will he be kicking or boxing?"

The Japanese Princess and the American Rebel

"Both. In a conventional kickboxing match, the fighters are required to make so many kicks per round. But because you are not a kickboxer, the rules of this match have been changed so that neither of you are required to make any kicks, or you can make as many as you like."

"And he will be barefoot?" I inquired.

"Yes, except for ankle wrapping, similar to your hand wrapping."

"And will I be barefoot also?"

"Only if you want to kick him back."

"I reckon I might as well keep my shoes."

"I agree," said Turtle.

"By the way, where is he allowed to kick?"

"Head, shoulders, arms, legs, stomach, and anywhere except your nuts."

"I've heard of them kicking in the nuts," I replied.

"Well if he does, he'll be disqualified, and you will win the fight," Turtle said as he burst out laughing along with everyone else.

"Wonderful! I get my nuts cracked and we win."

"Win any way you can, brother," he replied still laughing.

Then came the barrage of jokes.

"Hey, man, you might get to go home with a medical discharge from busted nuts. I wish I was in your place."

"Is this the same guy who trains by kicking down trees?"

"No that's another one. This one kicks a concrete block around for a soccer ball."

"Thanks for the encouragement, fellows," I said.

"Think nothing of it," said another, "We'll be with you all the way through the taps."

"Anyway," said Turtle, "it doesn't matter who he is. I've got a plan. Within the next two weeks we'll work up a strategy so you can whip the kickboxing champion of the world."

"Where is this guy from?" I asked.

"Let's see," he said, while looking at his list, "he is from our company. In fact he works in your platoon. His name is Ha Hyo Jun."

"Mr. Ha!" I exclaimed.

"You know him?" He asked.

"Yes, I work with him almost every day."

"What kind of person is he? Tell me something about him," Turtle said as his curiosity rose.

"Did you know that he was a kickboxer?"

"No, I never dreamed it. He is a little slender man of about thirty years of age, well mannered and polite. He is so...well you might say effeminate. There is nothing about him that seems like a fighter."

"Mmm," said Turtle, "the first thing you need to do is to put that out of your mind. You may not find him so nice and polite or effeminate in the ring. The first rule of fighting is never underestimate the enemy, in war and in the ring."

Turtle was right about our training, because in those two weeks, he had me training harder than I ever had in my life. Most of my sparring was with him, where he tried showing me how to cut the ring off to keep a fast opponent from using the whole ring, and then the use of body blows and uppercuts. Even though he was pulling punches, I got a good taste of his body blows and uppercuts. I saw then how impossible it would be for me to ever train enough to be even a poor match for someone like Turtle. Of course he was a professional, but he wasn't even rated among the top. Imagine what it would be like to fight a champion. I knew then I had just as well forget the fight game.

The night of the big event, I stood in my corner trembling like a dog in a veterinarian's office. I can't imagine anyone not being afraid and nervous before the first bell. In no fight was I ever calm before the bell. The only thing I have found to stop fear and nervousness is action. After the first engagement, like magic, all fear and nervousness are gone. The focus on your opponent takes over. You know his object is to destroy you, and yours is to destroy him. There you face him alone with nowhere to run, and nowhere to hide. There is no one to help you, not your trainer, not your friends, not even your mother. Everything is left up to you and you alone.

After the bell rings there is no time for planning or thinking. Your body and not your brain will now be in control. That is where your hard training comes in. Your arms, your legs, and your whole body act and react as they have been trained. Your focus is such that everything else fades away, even the roaring crowd. A part of your hearing tries to stay in touch with your trainer as he yells advice at you, but you miss most of that.

That night, all the matches were five rounds and mine was the third match. As I stood in my corner waiting for the announcement, Turtle was still coaching.

"Now remember, you are bigger and stronger than him, so you have to take the fight to him just as we trained. His only advantage is his kick, so nullify them like we trained."

Looking over at Mr. Ha, I noticed his ankles were wrapped as a boxer's hands and wrists would be. Proper wrapping of hands are very important, especially to a heavy hitter, to keep him from breaking bones. That thought only added to my fear. It made me wonder if Mr. Ha's kicks were so powerful that he had to wrap his feet and ankles to keep from breaking them. What else could he break? Maybe boards and cement blocks. At that time kickboxing was new to Americans. We knew a little about Ju Jitsu and Judo, but nothing about kickboxing. All we knew about it was some tall stories of broken boards, busted cement blocks, and sometimes broken necks. Turtle, of course, assured me he knew all about it, and with our strategy, a kickboxer wouldn't stand a chance against a boxer.

I stood there half listening and trying to believe Turtle, as I watched Mr. Ha stretch one leg straight up and then the other. He could easily put them in back of his neck.

How did I ever get into this predicament? I wondered.

Turtle was still talking, "Remember what I told you. According to the rules, once you touch gloves, the fight is on. Don't wait on him to come out of his traditional bow. If he is foolish enough to bow, go in and take his head off. It'll be legal according to the rules."

The referee called us out to ring center for instructions. We stood there face to face staring. However, I didn't stare him in the eyes. I had learned from Trusco Johnson at the Florence YMCA, not to do that. He said to pick a spot on the forehead to stare at. That way you could stare all day and still give the appearance of staring your opponent in the eyes, without any distractions. Even the opponent wouldn't know the difference. After the instructions, he sent us back to our corners, and the bell rang.

Round 1

We came out, touched gloves, and all fear and trembling disappeared. Mr. Ha stepped back, took his graceful bow, and I did exactly what Turtle told me *not* to do. I stepped back and bowed to him. We squared off, and before I knew it, Mr. Ha was all over me with a flurry of lefts and rights that completely threw me off guard, allowing him to make several kicks. He was much, much faster than I thought he would be. He used the whole ring to his advantage by ducking, weaving, crouching, and then seeming to disappear and to reappear somewhere else. He would get off a kick and back paddle before I could close with him. When I did manage to close, he was so adept at weaving his head and rolling with punches I made no real connection during the entire round. To his credit, he made four or five kicks and numerous combinations. The round was his, and I knew it.

While sitting in my corner after the round, Turtle started in on me.

"God dammit, you didn't do a damn thing like we trained. Instead of matching his silly bow, you should have taken his damn head off. And stop head hunting. It's too hard to hit. Stay close and work on his body. That'll slow him down. Listen up now. Are you listening? This guy is fast, but he can't hurt you except with his kicks, so you gotta crowd him. Stay close and he can't kick. Trade punches. You are the strongest."

Round 2

I rushed out and crowded him right away with left jabs, trying to make an opening for a right cross or hook, but his head movement was too good. The few times I made a connection to his head, he rolled with it, taking all the effect out. He managed several kicks, but I stayed close enough to make them ineffective.

Turtle's advice was beginning to sink in, and I stopped head hunting and concentrated on his body. By staying close it did eliminate his kicks, but he countered this with knee jabs to my legs and midsection, which was very telling. We were standing like that toe to toe when the bell rang. I knew it would be luck if that round was a draw.

The instant I sat down, Turtle started talking while working on a split over my eye. "You just now got it right. At the bell, rush out and before he is set, start on his midsection. He will give this time. Listen up now. Don't let him play over the ring. Cut it off like I showed you. Get him to the ropes, and when he goes left, you step left and drag your right foot. If he goes right, step right and drag your left foot. Cut his ring off. Keep him on the ropes. Work on his middle. He'll slow down. You are rolling your waist just right to keep his knee jabs from hurting. Keep it up."

Round 3

When the bell rang, I rushed out trying to meet him as far as possible toward the ropes, but he met me at ring center. There we took up where we had left off; head to head, me slugging and him kneeing. However, he soon gave and began backing up just as Turtle had predicted. Before long I had him close to the ropes, so his only escape was to slide by me either left or right. If he went left, I kept stepping left, and if he went right, I kept stepping right, all the while working on his body. The few times he did manage to slip by, I stayed on him until he was back toward the ropes. By cutting off his ring this way his kicks were almost nullified, and the body work had slowed him down until I was beginning to connect with his head. Then just before the bell, I caught his bobbing head with a solid left hook as it bobbed the wrong way, and down he went against the ropes. The bell rang as he slid down.

According to the rules, the bell couldn't save him, because he still had to rise before the count of ten. But that was no problem to him. He got right up and walked to his corner.

Round 4

We both rushed out and met at ring center. He was cautious now and tried his best to keep a distance and earn points with kicks. But Turtle's strategy was still working. I kept crowding him and found that elusive head much easier to hit, especially with short hooks and uppercuts. After a flurry of hooks and uppercuts, he went down. I skipped back to a neutral corner as the referee began his count. Mr. Ha slowly stood and upon completing the count, the referee wiped his gloves, looked him in the eyes and motioned for us to continue. Immediately, I connected with a left jab and then an overhand right that sent him back to the canvas for the count.

I always thought he shouldn't have been allowed to continue after the first knock down of that round, because he just seemed to stand there and wait on the final blow. I think the referee missed something when he looked in his eyes. Anyway, I was glad he wasn't hurt. But he was a real piss off because his bowing and graciousness took all the glory out of winning. He should have been some evil villain like Brutus or Snake, my childhood play enemies, or at least be faceless and nameless like the Indians I used to fight as a child. But that isn't the case in real life, because for every winner there is a loser. Later I wasn't certain who the winner was in our case. Mr. Ha had no visible bruises or marks, while I had two stitches in an eyebrow and a busted lip. Also it was two weeks before the soreness left my legs and ribs. Anyway, we remained the best of friends as long as we were together, and he remained my loyal love letter translator.

Chapter III
Back to Japan

The day finally came when the four of us, Ben, Dexter, Ernst, and I were leaving "The Land of the Morning Calm" and returning to "The Land of the Rising Sun." We returned on the same type LST ship that had brought us over, but this trip was nothing like the first. Instead of warm weather, it was freezing cold. Instead of calm seas, there were typhoon strength winds. Instead of sleeping on deck, we had to stay below with life jackets as waves washed over deck. Because this ship is almost flat-bottomed, it rides high on the water, and when the wave runs underneath, it comes banging down with a terrible crash. At times it seemed as if the ship would break in two, and in fact, they were known to do so in rough seas. I thought of how useless life jackets would be in that freezing water. Death from hypothermia would probably come in minutes.

However, we arrived in Kobe none the worse except for seasickness. I had been to other cities of Japan, even Yokohama and Tokyo, but I wasn't prepared for Kobe. It was the main drop off place for soldiers coming from Korea on R&R (rest and recuperation from combat). It was the place of recreation for all the armies of the United Nations who were fighting in Korea. There were Americans, British, Canadians, Australians, Turks, Greeks, Filipinos, and more.

All were there to be entertained, and the Japanese had prepared well for it. As far as could be seen were blocks and blocks of hotels, restaurants, and bars. The streets blared with western and oriental music, and the bars were full of the most gorgeous girls found anywhere in the world. A soldier could walk into any one of them and instantly be covered by the girls. At the time, prostitution was still legal in Japan and would be for several more years. In Kobe alone there was said to be ten thousand registered prostitutes controlled by ten men. This number didn't include the street walkers or unregistered ones.

This of course brought about a very real threat of venereal disease. In trying to curb its spread, the U.S. Army and the Japanese government worked together. One way of doing this was to assign every registered prostitute a VD card and VD number, similar to the G.I.s dog tag and serial number. On every sexual encounter, the girl was supposed to get the soldier's serial number, and the soldier was to get the girl's VD number. Then if the soldier caught any disease, he was to turn the girl's number in, and the Japanese man in charge of her was to have her treated. If the girl came up with a disease, she was to turn the soldier's serial number in, and of course, his company commander was to see to his treatment. I don't think this worked very well. I can imagine the complications of a girl turning in a dozen or more serial numbers, or a soldier turning in that many VD numbers. In fact, I never knew of a soldier giving or receiving a number, or one ever being asked for. With all this, the Japanese of Kobe were well prepared to send the men back to Korea, recuperated and broke, but not necessarily rested.

It was a most exciting place for a young man, and when I saw all this, my heart sank, especially when looking into the faces of my gang and seeing the hypnotic effect the place was having on them.

"Hey," I said, "don't forget we have to catch a train in the morning for Kure."

"Catch a train," bellowed Ben and Dexter at the same time, "Are you crazy?"

"You are kidding, aren't you?" Asked Ben.

I didn't say anything, but only looked at him and shook my head.

"Just look around," added Dexter, "You can't leave this place to go to a little rinky dink place like Kure and Eta Jima, can you?"

Ben, Dexter, and I argued back and forth. Ernst was neutral and had little to say. He had a girl in Kure to whom he had been writing, but he was like a sailor with one in every port. So he wasn't a problem, but he wasn't any help either.

We argued on the street until deciding to go in a bar and discuss it over a drink. That didn't help my position a bit, because the bar girls covered us. We were the only customers in the place with ten or twelve beautiful young ladies. They were dressed western, most in the popular split skirt or dress showing all leg and lots of thigh. There is no way Ben could ever again have recognized any of them by their face. To please the soldiers they even took American names such as Susie, or Marilyn, or if you liked, the name of your state-side sweetheart. I was having serious doubts about getting them out of there. I even began having doubts about getting me out.

We sat with our drinks and argued while the ladies went about their job of distracting us.

Finally, I said, "Okay, I don't blame you. Stay, but I'm going to Eta Jima."

"All right," said Ben, "let's go with the crazy damn Rebel. We can't trust the fool to go across a foreign country by himself. Without us, he would never find his way there, much less back."

So it was settled.

The next morning we left on the little train with the little wooden cars. The cars were equipped with straight back wooden seats and no cushions. We were used to a lot worse, so it didn't bother us a bit. The little coal-burning engine chugged, chugged out of the station, and soon, the train, like a giant snake, crawled over the hills, around the mountains and sometimes through them. When looking out the window, we saw that all available land was put to use. It was cultivated right up to the tracks, and even high up on the mountain slopes, plots were terraced out and planted. Very few automobiles or trucks were seen, but there were many scooters and three-wheeled small trucks. Japan is an extraordinarily beautiful mountainous country, and before long, all of us were enjoying the trip, even Ben. Ernst said, once we got him away from the girls, he would settle down and be all right.

The trains were always full of people, and we were a real curiosity to them. With their limited English, our no Japanese, and lots of sign language, we communicated pretty well. The Japanese are a friendly people and we laughed with them and had a really good time. Even having to change trains three times was no problem, because all we had to do was show our tickets and a trainman would put us on the right train.

We arrived at Kure at 9 PM and rented a room as our headquarters. As soon as we were settled, Ernst headed to see his girlfriend, and I went into the hotel bar with Ben and Dexter for a few drinks before going to the ferry. There they found their mates for the night. After a few drinks, it was 10 PM, and I knew I had to go because the last ferry left at 11 PM.

I walked outside, but there were no taxis. That was no problem though, because from where I stood, I could see the lit-up bay area below. I had walked it before, so I started in that direction. However, after descending a few blocks, I could no longer see the bay, and in the dark all the streets and buildings looked alike. Even the starlight was hidden by clouds, and the only light I had was a cigarette lighter. It was like being in a dark hole. Of course there was no one on the streets from whom I could get directions. I began to fear I was lost, when a much greater fear confronted me.

Like a ghost, the dim outline of a man suddenly appeared before me speaking in Japanese. It's amazing how reflexes take control of our moves in such fearful situations. Instantly I wanted to bring up my M-1, but not having it, I grabbed for my army 45 before realizing I didn't have that either.

Then I said, "No speak Japanese."

He spoke a few words in English, "Cigarettes, money."

Then suddenly from nowhere and with no sound, something jumped on my back and wrapped an arm tightly around my neck. I let out a terrified yell and began grabbling with the arm trying to pull it loose when the shadow in front closed in. I struck out at the shadow and felt my fist hit something solid.

During all this, I staggered back against either a stone wall or fence. The thing riding my back got the real blow, because it was between me and the wall. Because of the jolt his arm loosened, and I was able to shake him off.

I was free then, and I didn't hang around to see what it was all about. I ran into the dark not knowing or caring where I was going. After my take off, I did hear foot steps and Japanese voices, but not for long. It eventually dawned on me I should be running downhill, and I would eventually come out at the bay. I ran until my wind was gone, which I had plenty of back then, and I am sure the fright gave me lots more.

After I could run no longer, I stopped and stood bent over with my hands on my knees gasping for breath. While standing there I heard a sound like a diesel engine. I listened again and began following the sound and came out at a dock on the bay where a boat engine was running. The bay area was better lit, and after looking around I knew my ferry dock to be about a block away.

I arrived to catch the ferry with little time to spare. I sat down on the ferry still gasping and trembling from one of the most terrifying experiences of my life. I had visions of newspaper headlines reading, "American Soldier Found Floating In Kure Bay With Throat Slit."

When the ferry pulled up to the Eta Jima dock, the army shuttle bus was waiting. About a dozen soldiers got off the ferry and boarded the bus. I waited until last to board because I wanted to talk to the driver and have him let me off at Namiko's bar. It was almost midnight and if the bus took me on base, I may not be able to get through the gate because of the village curfew. So I stood by the driver and talked to him. I told him I had come from Korea, and we talked mostly about Korea. He had never been there, but feared he may soon have to go, so he had a lot of curiosity about it. When we approached the village, I told him where I wanted to get off.

"I am sorry," he said, "but I can't stop to let anyone off outside the base after midnight."

"But," I protested, "if I go through the gate, they may not let me out."

"I'm so sorry," he said in sincere sympathy, "but if I stop and let you off, I am in a lot of trouble."

I understood and knew there was no use to press the issue.

After the bus went through the gate and parked, we all got off. All the other soldiers headed toward their barracks, and I started walking toward the gate.

"Good luck," said the driver, as I walked off.

I knew I would need it. As I started through the gate, a military police corporal stepped in front of me.

"Hold it, Corporal," he said, "you are going the wrong way. You can't go out the gate after midnight."

"I'm not stationed here," I replied, "I'm from Korea," and showed him my papers.

He looked at them and then called his sergeant over, showing them to him. They looked at each other puzzled over a situation they had never encountered, probably wondering what a soldier stationed in Korea was doing on this side of Japan.

Finally the sergeant said, "I'm sorry, but we can't give anyone permission to go out the gate after midnight."

"Look, where am I going to sleep?" I asked. "I don't have a bunk here, but I do have a place to sleep in the village. I won't be on the street or in any bar."

Neither of them said anything. I knew then that they wouldn't give me permission because they couldn't.

"I came all the way from Korea for this, and I promise you will never see me again," I said, as I started walking off.

I knew they both sympathized with my situation, and they conveniently looked away as I hurried to the Cabana Bar.

When I walked into the Cabana, Namiko was standing behind the bar. She saw me and let out a very un-Japanese like scream and came running and jumped into my arms. We stood there clutching to each other as if afraid to let go. I had never seen her really cry, but now she was sobbing, and it made me cry.

Finally I was able to tell her I had to be out of the bar and off of the street before the MPs came by. She immediately began speaking in Japanese to her cousin and co-workers who had gathered around us. Her cousin replied something back.

Namiko looked up at me with her teary black eyes just sparkling, and said, "My cousin let us have her house. Do you remember where it is?"

Namiko no longer had our house. She had given it up when I went to Korea and moved back in with her family.

"Yes," I said.

"Key by door. Hurry before MP come. I be there at two."

She then stepped out on the street and then back in.

"No MP," she said, "hurry."

I hurried to the house which was about a half block away. I was anxious to get inside, because it was cold weather, and it had turned a lot colder in the last several hours. It had to be below freezing, and I was dressed in khakis and had no jacket.

When I reached the house, which was behind thick shrubbery, I knew I was safe from the MPs. It was cloudy enough so no star or moonlight came through as I searched for the key around the sliding glass doors. I felt all around the doors. No key. I went over the top, the bottom and both sides again and again. No key.

Where is the damn key? I wanted to holler.

I was so cold I began trembling. From time to time, I would give the search up, but the cold forced me back to it again and again. Going back to get Namiko was out of the question, because the MPs were steadily riding and walking by. Finally I gave the search up altogether and concentrated on trying to stay warm by doing push ups and other low profile exercises. I stayed low so the MPs wouldn't notice movement through the shrubbery. I even tried imagining I was in some hot place, but I still trembled from the cold.

Old crazy Ben Carr, as I sometimes called him, may not be the crazy one after all, I thought. Long about now, he would be full of whiskey and snuggled up warm and cozy. And here I was, hungry, thirsty, and freezing. Concerning the freezing part, I wondered if I would be entitled to any kind of medal for freezing to death at a girlfriend's door. I also wondered if any of the neighbors might call the MPs to report an American peeping Tom.

Yes, I had to be the crazy one to cross the ocean in a typhoon, leave all the gorgeous girls in Kobe, catch a train across a foreign country, expose myself to a mugging, risk being arrested by the military police, and now out in freezing weather in only shirt sleeves with no jacket. For what? For a little girl that didn't even weigh 100 pounds. It is strange the things that drive us.

When Namiko finally showed up to save me, she was startled to find me outside. But her surprise soon turned to sympathy when she realized how cold I was.

"Poor baby," she said as she retrieved the key from its hiding place, unlocked the door, and slid it open. We slid inside. Then she slipped her little wooden bottomed shoes off, knelt, took mine off, and placed both pair in the shoe place.

The heat didn't hit me in the face when the door was opened, because Japanese houses didn't have stoves or fireplaces. The heat came from a hibachi pot in which charcoal burned. It wasn't meant to heat the house, but was used to warm hands while sitting around and talking. For real warmth Japanese bundled up. Therefore, inside was almost as cold as outside. I knelt as close to the pot as I could without touching the hot coals. While kneeling there trembling, Namiko was busy putting warm bricks between the sheets to warm the bed.

Then she came over and said, "take clothes off. Hot tub warm you up quick."

"Are you going to scald me as soon as I get back?" I asked in a chattering voice.

She didn't laugh as she usually did when I picked at her about scalding me. I think she felt too guilty over me not getting into the house.

She did manage a smile, and said, "You know how I like to scald you. Now pull clothes off. Get in."

While feeling my face, she said, "You like ice. I so sorry."

That was one scalding I didn't mind, because I was too numb to feel it. And she was right. I did warm right up and was soon out, dry, and between the sheets with the warm bricks.

Before long, she had her scalding, and we both were warm and where we belonged. I then changed my mind about being crazy. This was worth much more than all my trials of getting here.

The next morning as we lay in bed, she said, "I have present for you."

"You have already given it to me," I said.

She looked at me puzzled for a moment, then broke out in a smile while pushing at me and saying, "Not that, bad boy. Besides we give each other present then."

"I show you," she said, as she reached over and presented me with a polished and bright bamboo tube, which was about eighteen inches long and three inches in diameter. It had a bright red cloth carrying strap tightly bound on it. Painted on it in English letters was written, "To My Beautiful Big American Rebel - the sun of my heart." I was puzzled as to what it was. I thought it must be a canteen with a shoulder strap. On seeing my puzzled look, she took it from me and showed me how the top slid open and handed it back. I opened it, looked in, and saw it contained a rolled paper, which turned out to be a painting.

The painting showed profiles of a Japanese girl and an American soldier. Their faces were close together as they looked intently into the eyes of the other. The faces were enclosed in a heart shaped border. Beneath the painting was a verse written in Japanese on her side and English on his side. The verse read as follows:

> There is a story that one time the sun was told
> there was a place of darkness on the earth.
> Since the sun had never seen darkness, he
> decided to go and find it.
>
> The sun searched and searched but never
> could find it, because wherever he went
> the darkness receded before his brightness.
>
> So he went back and reported there was
> no such thing as darkness because he
> had searched everywhere and could not
>   find it.

Beneath the verse was written:

> My Beautiful Big American Rebel,
> you are the sun in my heart
> and always will be.

The Japanese Princess and the American Rebel

Your Beautiful Little Japanese Princess
Namiko

I read it over several times before realizing the profiles were of us in perfect likeness, even to my little curl.

I then stammered, "That is us."

"Yes," she beamed.

I was so touched I couldn't speak. I looked at the painting and then at her. She could tell how surprised, touched, and pleased I was, so she watched me with her face aglow.

Looking proud, she said, "I wrote English also."

She had a right to be proud, because when I had left, she could only speak English in words and broken sentences and couldn't read or write any of the language. Now she spoke mostly complete sentences and could also read and write English.

She had learned all this, while I had learned nothing. Then she found time to do this beautiful painting, which from that moment became my most prized possession, only to be lost in Korea; but never to be lost in my memory and heart. What had I ever done to deserve the love of this wonderful woman?

After breakfast, I told her I had to go to Kure to get my duffle bag. In my rush to catch the ferry last night I didn't go back to the room to get it. It was a good thing I hadn't gone back for it, because if I had, the muggers would now have it, with all my worldly possessions.

"Good," she said. "We both go. We will see Aunt Mitchie, and I want to see Ben, Dexter, and Ernst. Also there is festival there today. It will be fun."

We were both dressed and ready in a short while. To my astonishment, she was dressed in dungarees (now called jeans), and twisting around like a model.

"You like? I dress like American girl for you today."

Yes, I did like. Her slim, firm, rounded hips were natural for jeans.

I picked her up and hugged her close, saying, "you better believe I like, but don't you dare change my perfect little Japanese princess into an American girl. Yes, I like them on you, but I also like them off."

She was puzzled at first by my meaning of also liking them off. Then when the meaning dawned on her, she let out the Japanese sound of exasperation and pushed back from me saying, "You so bad, but I love when you bad," then reached up and planted a long kiss on my lips.

Neither of us would let it go.

Later as we were getting dressed again, she pointed a finger at me, saying, "Don't you dare touch me or we never catch ferry."

On arriving at Hiroshima, our first stop was to see Aunt Mitchie. I was happy to see her, and she seemed happy to see me. Her husband wasn't home, and I was happy about that too. We had a very pleasant visit and when the time came to leave, Namiko went to the restroom. While she was gone, I asked Mitchie why Namiko didn't want to go see her mother or cousins, and if something was bothering her.

Mitchie looked to see that Namiko wasn't returning, and said, "I have to be at the Cabana Bar at noon tomorrow. Come by alone and we will talk."

After leaving Mitchie, we located Ben and Dexter with their girlfriends. They were as glad to see Namiko as she was to see them. They marveled at the way she looked in her jeans, and I still did too. Their girlfriends were really pretty, but against Namiko they were like two candles beside a spot light. We never did find Ernst, so we headed out on the city to enjoy the festival. There were parades with floats of all kinds. There were giant balloons, kites dragons, and many other things. There was certainly too much to take in in one day. In fact, the festival went on in different phases for more than a week.

We rented three rickshaws, which are wheeled vehicles carrying two people and pulled by a trotting man. Namiko and the girls would tell them where to go and off they would trot like a horse. Dexter and Ben kept wanting to have a three way race. Ben would bet his man-horse could out run ours, while Dexter kept yelling giddy-up and trying to get his date to yell it in Japanese.

So away the three Americans with their dates went, pulled around the city by their man-horses. They bought their pretty girlfriends anything their hearts desired and probably many things they didn't desire. We were certainly rich enough to do that. Why with combat pay, Dexter and I earned $145 a month. Ben was the poor one by earning only $130 a month. He should have been earning the same as we did, but every time he came up for a promotion, something beyond his control caused him to lose it. According to him, the cause was either Dexter, Ernst, or me.

It was a really fun time, without a serious word or thought throughout the day. Everything was just happy-go-lucky. The weather was pretty and not too cold. I was accompanied by the best friends anyone could have and the most lovely girl in the world, whom I loved with my very soul. To her, everything was a wonder and a glory. The floats and kites excited her. She was so happy in meeting and talking to her friends. She laughed to tears at the joking and playing between Ben, Dexter, and me. She seldom drank alcohol, but that day she indulged in the warm saki, which we all participated in heavily. We were so happy that day the thought came to me that if I never have another good day, life would have been worth living just for that one day. I still think that.

That night while riding back to the hotel, she was a little tipsy, but still happy and very talkative. We sat close and she kept reaching up for a kiss, saying over and over in perfect English, "I love you so very, very much."

The Japanese Princess and the American Rebel

I wouldn't have cared what language she used.

It was late the next morning before we caught the ferry back to the island, so it was about one o'clock before I got away from Namiko to meet Mitchie.

When I walked into the Cabana and took a seat, she came over and asked as an American woman would have, "What can I get you to drink, baby?"

"Coke," I replied, "I drank too much saki yesterday."

She smiled, left, and was shortly back, taking a seat.

"What is Namiko doing?" She asked.

"I left her in the yoga position doing her daily meditation."

"She is so conscientious about that, isn't she?"

"Very," I replied.

We sat for a while chitchatting, but I didn't leave Namiko to chitchat. I came to talk about her. So it wasn't long before I brought that to Mitchie's attention.

"I am sorry," she said, "for being so Japanese when talking to an American. You know there is a vast difference in the way the two races converse. The Japanese don't like confrontation, therefore, they are less direct and more evasive in speech than Americans. Sometimes you almost have to know the Japanese speaker to understand what he means by what he says. Americans say we talk in circles, and maybe we do. On the other hand, Americans speak more bluntly. They are more candid. So today, I am going to try being more American by speaking candidly. Namiko being my niece, I, of course, have known and loved her all her life. Since I have no children, she has always been like a daughter to me, as has her sisters Tokiko and Isora. Because of her personality and talent, I suppose we all expect too much of her. She has been, and is, the shining light or the star of the family. And she is so much in love with you. I think most of her thoughts are of you - day and night. When she speaks your name, her face just lights up."

"And I love her just as much," I replied.

"I know," she said with such a look of understanding, while placing her hand on mine. "I can see it in both of you, and I do sincerely sympathize with your position. However, that is not the way most of the family feels. Most are strictly against your relationship, especially my husband who is traditionally head of the family. Probably most Japanese men would be against it."

"Her mother too?" I asked.

"Yes," she answered and named only a few cousins about Namiko's age who were for us. "They have been against the relationship all along, especially when you started living together. However, they thought it would be over when you left for the war."

Then after a few moments of silence, with a laugh she said, "But to their horror you returned."

I didn't feel like laughing, but I did return a weak smile.

She continued by saying, "She is under a lot of pressure from the family, and being the obedient daughter she has always been, and loving her family the way she does puts her in a very disturbing way."

"You have never met her sisters, have you?" She asked.

"No."

"Have you ever wondered why?"

"Not really. I just assumed it was never convenient," I replied.

"Well you do know about the family living in Hiroshima when the bomb was dropped."

"Yes, Namiko told me about it. She told me about her father and brothers being killed and one sister injured."

"Isora was the one injured," she said.

"Did she tell you how seriously she was injured?'

"I remember her saying that she had been burned. That much of her clothes were burned off," I answered.

"It was much worse than that. Her face was disfigured so that it is beyond any real reconstruction. She lets no one see her face, except maybe Namiko. She wears a veil and spends all her time either at home or in the temple. I haven't seen her face since she was a child, and the truth is it still haunts me. When I think of it, the term monster comes to mind. Also this terrible disfigurement brings about a terrible emotional problem for her, which at times puts her in a bad state. When in one of these states, it seems that only Namiko can calm her. Namiko is her savior. If you have ever wondered why Namiko would sometimes have to go to her mother's home alone, it was because of Isora."

"An airplane or anything American can send her into one of her hysterical states, and Namiko has to come to her. I don't know what she would do without Namiko. Tokiko is not sick like Isora, but where Namiko has grown in Zen, so that it is impossible to hold hatred and bitterness, Tokiko is still filled with it and hates everything American."

"Oh, my God, I had no idea," was all I could say.

Putting her hand back on mine, she said sincerely, "I am so sorry to tell you this, but I knew that Namiko couldn't tell you."

"I never dreamed anything like that," I said, "but I can certainly understand their feelings. If the situation were reversed, I am sure I would feel as the sisters do. I would hate everything Japanese. I don't think I could ever forget and forgive as Namiko has."

Then I remembered that not too many years ago, I was busy in my play, killing the dirty little Japs and thinking they all should be wiped from the face of the earth. I also remembered the joy of hearing about the monster bomb destroying Hiroshima and of the misery it brought to the dirty little Japs.

The Japanese Princess and the American Rebel

Now that joy was gone and their misery had come home to me. Of course, none of this did I voice.

"I must tell you this," she went on, "then no more bad news, I promise. My husband has picked a young man he thinks Namiko should wed."

"What!" I exploded, really taken back by that. "How does Namiko feel about it? What does she say?"

She raised her hand to calm me, and then said, "She doesn't like it at all, and even refuses to listen when it is mentioned."

"And you?" I asked.

She reached over and put both hands on mine. Then said, "the first time I saw you, the day Namiko introduced you, I could see the bond between you. I could see the love you had for each other. Why anyone seeing the two of you together couldn't help but see it. You Americans would say it's a match made in heaven. We Buddhists (with Hindu influence) would say it's a rematching of souls. Namiko sincerely believes this is not your first meeting, nor will it be your last. I believe in this too."

"Please remember," she went on, "no matter what, don't ever doubt her love. The whole time you were gone, all she dreamed of and talked about was you. Why do you think she worked so hard on her English? It was for you. And do you have any idea how many hours after work and late at night she spent on that painting she did for you? By the way, what do you think of it?"

"It is the most precious gift I have ever received or ever dreamed of, and it will be my most treasured possession forever."

"She is a very talented person, isn't she?"

"I appreciate her more every day," I replied, "but you still haven't answered my question about how you feel about your husband's plans for Namiko."

"My feelings are that I want what's best for Namiko. But I honestly don't know what is best. I don't know what your intentions are. In fact I don't even know Namiko's intentions, because she has never discussed them with me. And it really doesn't matter what I or anyone else thinks, because it's a decision that the two of you will have to make. Furthermore, I believe it will be mostly your decision because I feel she will do anything you say. So what do you want?"

"What do I want? I want her! I want her more than anything in the world. I can't think or plan beyond her."

"Do you have a plan?" She asked.

That question was sort of like a wake-up slap. No, I didn't have a plan. I hadn't even thought about the complications of arranging for us to be together forever. I had just been living from day to day, enjoying our relationship. Feelings of the heart had completely overridden all logic. I had been living a dream that required no planning, so I didn't have a plan.

So my answer was a vague, "I want to take her home with me to the United States."

"When you go back to Korea, how long will you be there before being transferred back home?" She asked.

"About three months."

"Then you won't be coming back to Japan before going to your home?"

"No, I won't be able to."

"How long will you be in the army after getting home?"

"I will be discharged shortly after arriving in the States."

"Of course, you could then make the necessary arrangements to come back and get her. It happens quite often with American soldiers and Japanese girls, but there are lots of things to consider."

She went on, "Let's try to put our hearts aside and look at some facts to give the two of you something to think about. You know I have lived in the United States, mostly in California, and have traveled to some other states. However, I have never been to your state or any other southern state, so I know nothing of your part of the country. You might ponder on how Namiko would like your country. How would she be accepted there?"

She didn't say it, but for some reason, I got the feeling she had racism in mind.

"You have been on tours around Kure with her and I am sure you noticed how the people and her family love her, and how she loves and enjoys them. You have been to the temple with her and seen what a source of inspiration and strength it is to her. You know how the art gallery and her painting excites her. And now you know about her sisters. You know how terrible it would be for Isora to be deprived of her."

She looked down at her hands resting on the table for a long time, then continued.

"What it boils down to for you to get married is doing one of two things: Namiko giving up these things to move to the United States or you giving up what you have in the United States to move to Japan. The question: even with the strong love you have for each other, would she be happy in the United States, would you be happy in Japan?

You see, from logic, it is really simple, but when hearts are involved, it becomes very complicated. And I am enough of a romantic to believe that often times our hearts make more *damn* sense than our logic.

"I'll say one more thing," she said, but had to stop to compose herself, because she was about to cry. "The decision is yours and Namiko's, not mine, not her mother's, not my husband's, and I would be happy and proud to have you in the family," she said.

Looking at her, I realized what a wise and compassionate woman she was. It was so obvious she and Namiko were related.

I said to her in all sincerity, "Thank you so very, very much, and I would be proud to call you Aunt Mitchie." We were both teary-eyed.

While sitting and reflecting on the things she had said, I was suddenly hit by the realization of the heartache I had brought to this fine Japanese family. I could then see clearly how upsetting I had been to their orderly life. This was a family of close ties. It was a family from a nation that had bound families together through thousands of years of tradition and culture. The tragic war had, of course, been a big disruption to the family in many ways other than the deaths of so many; but they had pulled through and were probably closer than ever. Then along came this soldier from the enemy's army who stole the heart of the family star. He not only stole her heart but wants to take her away to the other side of the world, and she seems so anxious to go. And to make it worse, it's not even a civilized country like Japan, but a country where people of all races are all mixed together. It was a country only two hundred years old versus Japan's two thousand. It wasn't even old enough to have a trace of culture. With this realization, I could envision the pressure that had been on Namiko, and was still on her. Yet my Little Princess never gave me a clue, but chose to bear it alone.

I thought of how Namiko had grown up in this rich environment of loving family and friends. I thought of the city, the bay, and the island she loved so much. I thought of the temple and her religion which so inspired her, and I thought of her painting which was definitely inspired by all of this. This rich environment was like a rich garden, and she was the beautiful flower growing from it.

I couldn't imagine her growing and thriving anywhere else, especially in my little red neck southern town - population two thousand. For most of those residents, anyone living twenty miles away was a foreigner. So I could imagine what a real foreigner Namiko would be, especially being so different from them. I thanked God for that in many ways. But, I am not putting the people of the town down, because they were wonderful people in many ways. They just weren't ready for a foreign invasion. Not even of one.

In my town, she wouldn't have the closeness of family or the children and friends meeting her on the streets. There would be no regular little fun festivals to fill the town with excitement. Nor would there be refreshing ferry rides over the bay to her beloved island, where she could hike up to our waterfall. There would be no beach she could walk in search of the seashell of forgetfulness. She wouldn't have her temple with its uncluttered beauty of quietness and simplicity that so inspired her. However, there were five churches in my town, and I am sure any one of the preachers would be more than glad to save her soul from her heathen ways.

Suddenly with heart-breaking realization, I knew this little flower which had grown so bright and beautiful, if transplanted to my garden, would surely wilt and die.

Even if all these obstacles could miraculously be overcome, there remained the impossible one—Isora. Then I thought about living in Japan. But my family was just as close and precious to me as hers was to her.

What would I do in Japan? How would I make a living? I was in excellent physical condition. I could trot all day, so I might get a job pulling people around on a rickshaw. Then it would be my luck for Ben and Dexter to show up and rent me for a race. No, I wouldn't fit in her country any more than she would fit in mine. And there would still be the problem of Isora.

After our conversation, I needed more than a Coke. In fact, I needed to get drunk, and I did. I went to several other bars, and when I got home it was late. Namiko met me with her usual bright smile and kiss.

Then she said, "I love you. I miss you. Where you been? Dinner cold." Observing me closer, she said, "you drunk. Why?"

The alcohol having a firm hold on my tongue, I slurred out, "Hold on. That is five or six questions at once."

Looking thoughtful and counting on her fingers, her quick mind brought a quick response, saying, "No, four statements, two questions. Now answer."

"Okay," I replied, "I was talking to Aunt Mitchie, and it saddened me."

On hearing that, the look on her face was a complex one of shock, sadness, and despair.

"What are we to do?" I asked. "Why didn't you tell me about your sisters and the heartache I have caused you?"

She stood looking at me with tears starting to run down her cheeks, saying nothing. She didn't have to say anything because we were communicating without words, as we often did. I could feel her moods and almost read her thoughts as she could read mine. It was as if we had known each other forever, communicating like twins are said to be able to do.

Finally she said, while pulling my hand, "I am sorry. Come, let's sit down and talk now."

We sat down and she continued, "I didn't tell because I was afraid, afraid of how it might affect you, afraid it might rob us of some happiness."

"But you bore the burden alone," I replied, "You should have let me share it with you."

"I know, but I want so much for you to be happy. This has been the happiest part of my life, and I didn't want anything to bother it."

Cupping her face in my hands and kissing her, I said, "My precious little princess, nothing could ever bother my love for you and I mean nothing."

She snuggled close and put her head against my chest. Then said, "I don't know what to do. I pray every day for things to be right for us, and I pray every day for Isora and Tokiko. Tokiko can do all right without me, but Isora may be some better, but still needs me so."

We went over our situation from every angle and talked until the wee hours of morning. She did most of the talking, because she needed to. She had been carrying so much for so long I knew it would do her good to share it. So I gladly listened with my heart almost bursting with love for this brave little girl. And at the same time almost breaking from fear that our love could never be fulfilled.

After the talking and crying had wound down, she said in essence, and I agreed, that what ever happens is left up to God. He has given us each other for a part of our lives and that is a blessing in itself, and He may see fit to give us each other for the remainder of our lives; but regardless of what happens, all we can do is to enjoy each other for as long as we can.

Then to lighten things up, she jokingly said, "You stay gone all evening. I think maybe you butterfly."

What the Japanese girls meant by "butterfly" was a boyfriend going from girl to girl as a butterfly goes from flower to flower.

Pulling her close in a tight hug, I said, "No, no, little flower, you are the only flower for this butterfly."

"I know," she replied, in a giggle, "and I am no flower for any other butterfly."

Then she added with another American term she had picked up, "And you better believe it."

"Now," she said, "I warm cold dinner. Then we find something more fun to do." Then she burst out in her infectious laugh, saying, "As soon as you get scalded."

After our scalding we lay close as I ran my hand over her firm little stomach. I knew better but I asked anyway. "You are not pregnant, are you?"

She looked at me with her sparkling eyes and asked, "Would you want me to be?"

"Yes," I answered, "would you want to be?"

Smiling and placing both hands on mine which still lay on her stomach, she said, "Oh yes, yes, yes, yes. It would be wonderful. It would be wonderful to feel it grow, knowing it to be part of you. It would be ours and no matter what happened, I always have part of you. But no, I'm not."

Then with eyes wide with her devilish look, she said, "Maybe try harder."

"I don't think we could try any harder," I said, "but we can certainly keep on trying."

"Come," she said, pulling me over to her, "now is perfect time."

Then all our troubles were gone. Troubles couldn't follow us to our magic world of oneness. There was no room for troubles there, because it was full of sacrifice and happiness. It was a very unselfish world where self was seldom thought of. It was a world where our only desire and need was to please the other. In return for this unselfish sacrifice, each was rewarded a heavenly pleasure. With this pleasure we were taken beyond all bounds of reality where passions and dreams unite. United there our souls melted together in complete contentment. If that is not religion, it is close enough for me.

Later we lay fitted like two spoons. Nothing is so wonderful as the peace and contentment that comes with the exhaustion of passionate lovemaking. You can be too exhausted to speak while gasping for breath with muscles twitching, but still that wonderful feeling of peace and fulfillment is there. I lay in that state with my face buried in her hair feeling the little twitches of her body. The muscle spasms going on for a while, gradually slowing to a stop. Then I knew by the stillness of her body and her deep even breathing that she had dozed off, and slept in peace and fulfillment.

I didn't go to sleep for a long time. I hadn't learned to take things by faith and relax as she had. Maybe I should have paid more attention when she tried introducing me to meditation. But I hadn't, so I lay awake with many things running through my mind. I thought of what she said after our long talk.

"Let's think no sad thoughts, but only happy ones. Let's enjoy the days we have left. Let's pray for many more, but be happy with the ones we have."

That was a big order. Apparently it was not a big order for her, but it certainly was for me.

I hugged her even closer, thinking, and wondering about our love. It was of sex and passion for sure, and in plenty, but it went far beyond that. I felt sure that if sex was never again to be a part of it, I would still want to be with her, just to hold her, and feel the closeness of her. I felt so incomplete without her. It was as if I were a half circle and she the other half.

I also wondered, with all the pretty girls in Kobe (thousands of them), why did I have to make my way across the country to be with this one? With all the girls I had known in the United States, Japan and Korea, why was I so drawn to her? Some girls I had really liked and felt a strong attachment to, but none were even close enough to compare to this relationship. I knew there must be several billion women in the world, and I wondered if somewhere in those billions, her replacement could be found. I thought not. Maybe we are entitled to only one real love with all others being poor substitutes. All these thoughts went through my mind until daylight when I went off to sleep, trading the troubling thoughts for troubling dreams.

I often think back and realize that from that little Japanese girl, I learned more about unselfish love and strength than I have from anyone. Every time I feel down or depressed or want to complain about something, her picture comes to mind. The picture I see is a little girl facing the horror of seeing her city destroyed, most of her family and friends killed, her older brother flying his plane into an enemy ship, then the feared enemy occupying her homeland. Some way she found the faith and strength to overcome all this and to grow in spirit until her heart was free of all hatred and bitterness, which gave her the purest love and zest for life I have ever known. She is my hero and always will be. In so many ways, she is still the wind beneath my wings.

After that night I only had five days left, so we were hardly apart for more than a few minutes except for one night when Namiko had to go to Isora during one of her bad days. During that time, we only made two trips to Kure: one was to go with the gang to the English club to see if any of the old crowd was there. The only ones we knew were Big York and a few other Australians. All the others were recent arrivals. However, it was good to see the ones we knew, and we had a good visit.

We spent the remainder of our time on the island just being together. That time together seemed to be all we needed. We did as we agreed: mentioned no sad things and tried to think no sad thoughts. However, the nearer the time drew, the harder it became not to think sad thoughts.

When the day came, it definitely wasn't a good day. In fact, it was one of the hardest days of my life, and it became impossible for either of us to keep the spirits of the other up. We tried, but it couldn't be done, because in our minds we felt it would be our final goodbye. In our hearts we hoped and prayed it wouldn't be.

The time spent packing my duffle bag was quiet. Neither of us spoke. We put off going until the last ferry of the night. Then when it was time, I put my duffle bag on one shoulder and hung my prized painting in the bamboo case on the other, and we caught a taxi to the ferry. When we arrived at the dock, we had about twenty minutes before the ferry left—our last twenty minutes. I paid the taxi driver and Namiko told him to wait for her.

It was a full moon night with a chilly breeze from the bay. The moonbeams tumbled all around and sparkled and bounced over the water. It was a beautiful night. In fact, it was identical to the full moon night when we had stood in the school garden by the bay as she christened me "My Beautiful Big American Rebel" and then declared her love to me, and I declared mine to her. That night was the beginning of our love. Could this night which looked so much like the other be the ending?

We stood in the moonlight hugged close together, with coat collars turned up to ward off the chilly breeze. I looked down into her face as she looked up into mine, like the picture hanging on my shoulder, as that thought suddenly crossed my mind.

She suddenly said, "You will always be the sun in my heart."

It was so eerie that she should come out with the very words written beneath the picture at the same time my mind was filled with it. It was as if we both were looking at it. Had she looked into my mind, seeing the same picture and then voiced the words beneath it? Or had she painted the picture of our final goodbye from some unconscious premonition? I wondered then and have wondered ever since.

Finally I managed to speak, and said, "Namiko, my little princess, my dear little princess, how I do love you and always will love you."

She tried to speak, but broke into a sob. Then composed herself enough to say, "You know we are meant for each other. You know we should be together. I don't know…what…I can't…"

Whatever it was she was trying to say, she couldn't finish because she broke down crying.

"I know we belong together, and in some way we will be," I said.

She couldn't seem to stop crying, and the tears were freely running down her cheeks and mine were too. I cupped her little face in my hands and tried kissing the tears away. We stood there with our faces together, both crying while our tears mingled together as our hearts had.

As we stood there crying and brokenhearted, someone hollered to board the ferry. We had been standing close to the loading plank, and I walked backwards on it still holding her hands until forced to let go.

While I stood on deck, she spoke loud and clear, "My darling, I love you, and you will always be in my heart."

Before I could respond, the two diesel engines roared to life and shoved the ferry out into the night, out into the darkness away from the light of my heart. Even though she couldn't hear, I spoke out into the noise and the darkness.

"Namiko, my beautiful little Japanese princess, I love you, and you will always be in my heart."

And she has been in my heart for over forty years.

Chapter IV
Afterwards

That night I felt I had left my reason for living on the Island of Eta Jima, arriving at Kure as sad and miserable as anyone could be. When docked, I took a taxi and was shortly at the hotel. I entered the room to find the gang all excited from news received that we had been granted an extra day. We didn't have to leave until the day after tomorrow. They were all excited over the extra day, and I would have been too under different circumstances.

Ben looked at me with a pleading and hopeful look, asking, "You are not going back to the island, are you Reb?"

I reflected back on our heart-wrenching goodbye and thought, Oh God, I just couldn't go through that again, and Namiko certainly shouldn't have to. So with those thoughts, I said, "No, no I'm not."

"Good," everyone yelled in unison.

"Now we can pitch a last night's party together," said Dexter.

"And have tomorrow to get over it," added Ernst in his pragmatic way.

"Let's get on with it," I said.

So out into the exciting nightlife of Kure went four excited happy-go-lucky young American soldiers—that is, except for one. They were young and healthy and full of energy and vigor, determined not to leave an uncorked bottle or unscrewed woman in Kure. They weren't alone, for the streets were full of such men from armies of numerous countries. From this mixture of nationalities, conversations could be heard in many languages as a mixture of western and oriental music blared from the bars. It was an exciting place and an exciting age for the young men. Gaiety and laughter were everywhere. In fact, there were celebrations still going on from the big festival that Namiko, Dexter, Ben, and I had participated in with our man-horses.

For this festival, the Japanese were walking the streets celebrating with sparklers and little harmless firecrackers that could be held in hand without injury. As we walked in the midst of this celebration, we met a group of girls who began throwing little firecrackers in our direction. As I looked at the girls, one of them looked at me, and our eyes locked in surprise.

"Carl," she said, and threw herself in my arms.

It was Otsu, the first girl I had met when arriving in Kure. It was hard to think of her as Japanese. Due to her fiery passion and temper, she seemed more Italian or Mexican than Japanese. She was bigger than most Japanese women, and because of this and her temper, she dominated the girls around her. She always had a following of girls, so I could always depend on her to provide my buddies with dates. She wore her hair short. Her teeth protruded just enough to give her a pretty mouth and smile. She was tall for a Japanese, and had a very well-developed body with big breasts, which most Japanese women didn't have. She was a very attractive girl. She spoke good English, probably from the many American service men she had known, and was a real party animal who loved to get right in and cut up with the guys. She also loved the American Tom Collins as well as her Japanese saki.

The night we met was my first day on land after a twenty-one day horrible sea voyage of sea sickness. She took me home with her that night, and the next morning she was steadily talking as she usually was. My hangover was too big to do more than listen, so it was mostly a one way conversation.

"You stay with me here when off duty, okay?" she said.

"Maybe."

"Maybe nothing, you stay, okay?"

"We'll see."

"Nice place, nice girls stay in other rooms. You bring friends to see them," she insisted.

"Okay," I said, hoping she would hush.

"Good. You not be sorry," she said, putting her arm over me, and snuggling up.

Then she asked, "How many times?"

"How many times what?" I asked.

"You know, how many times last night?"

"I don't know."

"Six," she exclaimed while sitting up and holding up six fingers!

"Aw, come on."

"Yes, six," she insisted, while smiling excitedly.

"No, you miscounted."

"No, no, no miscount," she said, "maybe do seven."

"No, I got a bad headache," I said while pulling away.

But that was like pouring gasoline on a fire to put it out.

"Yes," she said, rolling over on me, "do seven, make head better." I knew then I was in for a wild time with that woman, and I was. I did stay with her, and she was as good as her word. She always provided a date for anyone I took with me. Sometimes I took Ben, Dexter, Ernst, Terry, Willis, Buck, and others over from the island for some wild weekends. This went on until I met Namiko, and somehow Otsu found out about her. That threw her into one of her rages, and she threatened to kill me with a butcher knife. She ran me, Terry, and Buck around wielding it for a while, until we were able to overcome her and take it. Luckily the only thing cut was my shirt and Terry's finger. Even after taking the knife she still raved. Finally I took her and her rage to bed where it was eventually expended.

I didn't see her but two times after that. The last time I saw her, she told me she had something to show me, and commenced pulling her blouse and bra off. As she stood topless, she pointed to her left breast.

"See," she said, "I always have you close to my heart."

On her breast was tattooed "Carl L. Porter, Jr. class of 52." She had it done from a graduation card I had given her. That was the last time I saw her until now. I was really glad to see her though, as were Ben, Dexter, and Ernst. We had some good times together and she had been straight with all of us. She was a very fun and likeable person.

"When you come back?" She asked. "I thought you in Korea. Think maybe you dead."

"No, I'm not dead, but very much alive and here until day after tomorrow. You weren't wishing I was dead were you?"

"No, no," she exclaimed, "I'm glad to see you," then planting a kiss on my lips.

"Well, I'm glad to see you too."

"And you here for tonight and tomorrow?" She asked.

"Yes."

"Good, then let's bar hop and get drunk," she yelled, while kissing and holding me tight.

"Why not," I said, "let's go."

And off we went, not having to worry about girlfriends because Otsu had her usual group with her. There were even two extras, which Ben immediately claimed, giving him three.

"Hell no," said Dexter, "You get two and I get two."

"You don't need two," argued Ben, "Hell you probably don't even need one."

They went on for a big part of the night fussing over the extras.

I downed so much alcohol that night I was robbed early of memory. I had just reached the enlightened stage of life where I had found the answer to all problems and heartaches—alcohol. Just down enough of it and all problems would be gone. It was my seashell of forgetfulness. I held on to that belief for a long time—way too long in fact. It was a long time before I realized that alcohol is like a pain pill, only dulling the pain, and allowing it to come back with a fury. It never cures it, and eventually even fails to dull it, while bringing on pains of its own.

The next morning, I could only recall confused bits of the night. A little memory here and a little there, but nothing to make a whole. I do though, to this day, remember waking with the most awful hangover and headache I have ever had. I had quite a few hangovers, but never anything like this one. I awoke groaning and reached up to hold my head together, because I expected it to explode any minute. It was even sore to the touch. I had never had a hangover to make my head sore. Then after further exploration I found a bandage over my eye. I turned my head and there was Otsu lying beside me, looking at me in a concerned way. I noticed she was fully dressed. In fact I was too.

When she saw my eyes open, she asked, "You okay?"

"Except for this God awful headache."

"I worried, think maybe you hurt bad."

"Why should I be hurt, and why is this bandage over my eye?"

"You look hurt," she said, and reached over picked up a mirror and handed it to me.

I took it and saw a face staring at me I hardly recognized. The face had an eye nearly swollen closed with a bandage over it. It had split lips with scrapes and bruises all over.

"What in hell did you do to me?" I yelled.

"I do nothing," she replied, then burst out laughing as if it was funny. "You don't remember?" she asked.

"Remember what?"

"You fight Big York."

"Big York! I must have been crazy drunk to fight that monster."

Big York was one of our Australian buddies we had met at school. He was a sergeant and veteran of ten years and had fought the Japanese through the jungles of Indonesia throughout the war. He stood about six-foot four and weighed about 220 or 230 pounds. He seemed to be nothing but shoulders, arms, and nose. Otsu couldn't stop laughing.

"What's so funny?" I asked.

"You think I do that," she finally got out between peals of laughter. "At one time I wanted to. But now, I only love, not hurt you." When she finally got over her laughing spell, she said, "I already go out and get milk, tea, ham, and Coke. What you want?"

"Nothing yet. Why were we fighting?"

"I don't know. Everybody drunk. But I think you start. You hit him. His nose bleed bad. You too drunk to stand, much less fight. Then he keep knocking you down. You keep getting up. Every time he knock you down, he say 'Stay down, Yank.' But you get back up. Finally Ben and Dexter jump on you and hold you down. You still try to get up. Ben say 'Fight's over you damn hard headed Rebel. It's time to quit.'

"Then Big York say, 'Thank ye, mates, I was getting a little tired. That is one hard-headed Yank.'

"Then while Ben and Dexter hold you back, you yell back at Big York, 'I'm no damn Yankee. I'm a Rebel.'

"'Whatever you say, Yank,' was Big York's reply.

"Then everybody get okay. Big York call one of their medics and he put bandage on eye."

About that time the gang entered loud and boisterous as ever, ready to celebrate our last day.

"Howdy, Champ, ready for a few more rounds?" Ben asked as he chuckled.

"Champ, chump from what Namiko, I mean, Otsu tells me," I replied, while glancing toward Otsu hoping she hadn't caught the slip of tongue.

She did, however, and glared at me shaking her fist, saying, "I finish what Big York start."

The gang enjoyed that and jumped right in encouraging her.

"Go ahead, Otsu. Show us how it's done. Work on his good eye."

"Jump on him while he's down."

"You'll hush," I yelled, "you know how crazy she is without encouraging her."

"Me crazy!" she exclaimed, still laughing, "but not crazy enough to keep getting up to be knocked down again and again."

Dexter came in saying, "Don't feel bad, Reb, you should see Big York. Boy you really put the hurt on him. Why his fist is all skinned up."

Everybody burst out laughing. It was my turn in the barrel and not Ben's, so they went on and on with Otsu gleefully enjoying it.

Finally tiring of tormenting me, Ben handed me a glass of scotch and Coke, saying, "Here, this will perk you up so we can use up our last day."

After a few of those I was beginning to feel that I might make it, and I said that I was probably as ready to go as I would ever be.

"Well let's be on our way," said Dexter.

"Oh no," objected Otsu, "he can't go yet. I not through with him."

"Not through with him, why he's too beat up to be any good," replied Dexter.

"Oh no," she said looking over at them with a sly mischievous smile. "Only head hurt, don't need head. He fine everywhere else. I already check. If Big York hurt more than head, he have to fight me," she giggled.

This was her thing, and she was enjoying my embarrassment tremendously.

Looking at them with a devilish look, while pretending to undress, she said, "Come back in maybe two, three hour, maybe I be through then."

"Okay, we'll check by later," one of them said as they walked toward the door.

"Wait a minute," I hollered, "you can't leave me here in this condition with this wild woman. I'm hurt. I'm sore."

"That's okay, honey," soothed Otsu, "I be easy and promise not to hurt you."

As they walked out of the room laughing, all of them, including Otsu, were really enjoying themselves.

Before long, she had me enjoying it too. And you know she still had that tattoo.

After a little time and several more drinks, my head was feeling much better as we lay on the bed talking. Of course, as it had always been, she did most of the talking, and I did most of the listening.

"So tomorrow you go back to Korea?" She asked.

"Yes."

"War over, you should soon go home."

"In about three months."

"What you do then?"

"Probably go back to work at the railroad, or go to school."

"Go to school to learn what?"

"To become a veterinarian. An animal doctor."

"A what?" She said astonished.

"Animal doctor. A person who treats animals when they are sick."

She burst out laughing, saying, "You joke."

"No, no joke."

"You mean in America, there are people to doctor animals?"

"Yes."

She thought that to be so funny she laughed so hard until it had me laughing.

"I always want to go to America, now I really want to go to a place where they even have animal doctors. People should never get sick there. But why you want to doctor animals and not people?"

"I like animals."

"Better than people?"

"Probably."

"You very strange person," she said, placing her hands on my face and giving me a big kiss. "I must be strange too to love such a strange man. But if you take me to America I learn to help doctor animals. Two strange people together be good."

She really wanted to go to the United States, and in the past she had often hinted and on several times outright asked me to take her home as a wife, which is the only way I could have taken her. I made no answer to her new proposal and she continued.

"You never find a better wife than me. I know how to treat a man and please him. Don't you think so?"

"You most certainly do."

"Then why you not want me?"

"It's not a matter of not wanting you. It's just that I can't take you with me because I am not going home on my boat, but the U.S. Navy is taking me home."

"I know that," she said, with an aggravated look. "You could come back to get me as other Americans come back to get wives. I know I not been real good girl, but when your wife and in America I be perfect. I promise. You never be sorry."

"I know you would," I said, "and when I get back we will write to each other and talk about it."

"Bullshit, when you leave I never hear from you again. You never write to me from Korea before."

"Tell me something, Otsu, why do you want so badly to go to the United States? I know it's not just to go with me."

"I rather go with you than anyone I know, but I would go any way I can. Life in United States should be so much better. There I wouldn't have to sleep with men for money."

"Why do you have to in Japan?" I asked.

"Why? What else can I do?"

"What about your family? Can't you stay with them?" I asked.

"My family!" She said with a snarl I didn't know she to be capable of making.

Then she told me the story of her family.

Her mother and father were poor farmers living outside of Kure, and she was an only child. During the war her father was killed, and her mother married a widower who had a son and daughter. After marriage they had two children, which gave them a family of five children. Otsu never felt like she was a part of the family. Her stepfather was abusive to her and favored his children over her. Her older stepbrother raped her numerous times, and her stepfather and her mother either disbelieved or ignored it. Finally the stepfather tried to marry her off to an older man. The night before she was to be wed, she slipped out of the house and made her way to the city of Kure where she remained.

I never knew her story until then. I suppose people are people whether Japanese, American, or whatever nationality, and all have dysfunctional families. That term however wasn't used back then. Messed-up or screwed-up was the proper term. On learning her story and knowing how badly she wanted to go to the United States and how simple it would be to arrange, Namiko came to mind. Oh why couldn't they change places? Why couldn't Namiko have been from such a screwed-up family instead of such a close-knit one. But if she had, she probably wouldn't be the little princess I loved so.

Later during the day, we all decided to go to the English club. As we walked in, Big York saw us and came to meet us.

"Hey Yanks," he said. Then looking at me and sticking out his hand, he said, "How's my favorite Yank today?"

"Have been better," I said.

"You don't look bad," he replied.

"Where are your bruises?" I asked.

"You laid a good one on my nose," he said, pointing to it.

"There is no way I could've missed that big snout."

"Come on, Reb," whispered Ben, "don't start again."

"Next time, Yank, don't be so drunk," Big York said.

"I'm not drunk now," I said.

"Oh no," said Dexter.

Then I finished before Dexter could interrupt.

"But if I'm ever crazy enough to fight you again, I'll at least have a baseball bat."

Big York burst out in his big laugh, reaching around my shoulder, nearly lifting me off the floor, and said, "You are all right, Yank, come on let's get a drink."

"I'm not a Yank, I'm a Rebel."

"Whatever you say, Yank."

We all walked to the bar.

We spent the rest of the evening in the club, and not once did they let us buy a drink. It was a most heart-warming evening with true mates. It has long been a custom with the British and Australians on special occasions such as New Year's Eve or the parting of friends, to gather and sing "Auld Lang Syne." The song was written by Robert Burns in 1788 in his Scottish dialect, and there is no poem or song more heart-wrenching than this, especially when sung by the British or Australians.

So when the time came to leave, one of the piano-playing Aussies said, "Come on, mates, it's time to sing the Yanks away."

We all gathered around the piano.

Big York had one arm around me and one around Ben when he said, "I've already sang you Yanks off one time, but you keep coming back," then broke out in his loud laugh. The piano began and the drunken voices started singing:

>Should Auld acquaintance be forgot
>   And never brought to mind?
>Should auld acquaintance be forgot
>   And auld lang syne!

Chorus
For auld lang syne, my jo,
    For auld lang syne,
We'll tak a cup o' kindness yet,
    For auld lang syne.

And surely ye'll be your pint stowp!
    And surely I'll be mine!
And we'll tak a cup o' kindness yet,
    For auld lang syne.
    For auld, &c.
We twa hae run about the braes,
    And pou'd the gowans fine;
But we've wander'd mony a weary fitt,
    Sin auld lang syne.
    For auld, &c.

We twa hae paidl'd in the burn,
    Frae morning sun til dine;
But seas between us braid hae roar'd
    Sin auld lang syne.
    For auld, &c.

And there's a hand, my trusty fiere!
    And gie's a hand o' thine!
And we'll tak a right gude-willie-waught,
    For auld lang syne.

The next morning we left Kure for Kobe and back to Korea.

Chapter V
Return to Korea and Back Home

I left Japan broken-hearted, only to arrive in Korea to face another tragedy. James was no longer with us. He had faced the war from the first to the last. He had survived the wet muddy foxholes of the south and tied the frozen bodies of his buddies to gun barrels in bringing them out of the frozen mountains. No soldier had survived more than he had. Through all of this, he went unscathed, except for losing a chunk of his ass. Then the war ended, and he wasn't among the 33,629 dead. The gods had been with him. He had beaten all the odds.

Then one bright sunny day, a beautiful day, the kind of day that makes one doubt the reality of death, he was trying to unload a misfired mortar shell when it decided to go off and take part of his head with it.

Why? Why? I kept asking, but found no answer. After having faced so much, why was he cut down for no reason? Why would fate or God or Buddha or whatever controlled such things allow that to happen? Maybe Namiko or my Christian grandmother, with their wonderful faith, could accept such things and find peace in it; but I seemed to be a long way from being able to see any light in such darkness. A verse from a poem of which I cannot remember the author's name came to mind: "Every path leads but to the grave." Then in three months, I lost the rest of my gang when Dexter and I boarded the ship for home. That left me with a gang of two, and soon Dexter would be gone from my life forever.

I mentioned earlier that two of my most vivid memories of Korea are the first and last day. The last was somewhat like the first in that the ugly hills were still there, but they somehow looked different. The smell of the country was still there, but somehow it was not so offensive. I was happy to be leaving and going home, but somehow I was sad.

The night before sailing, Dexter and I went on top deck and watched the remains of American soldiers being loaded. The flag-draped coffins were lined up on the dock with a soldier standing by. When the ship's crane swung

The Japanese Princess and the American Rebel

around, he would place a sling around a coffin and stand at attention with a salute as it was swung around and lowered into the ship's deep belly. Down below, a sailor would free the sling and secure the coffin for a safe trip home. I counted over two hundred coffins being loaded before I went below and to bed. I don't know how long the loading went on. Later I heard there were two thousand coffins below, which was about the same number going home to be discharged or reassigned. All were going home to family and friends, half to a happy reunion, half to a sad one. I knew Dexter and a few more of the ones above. I wondered if I knew any of the ones below. I wondered if Buck or James may be among them. Buck and I came over together. We may be going back together. I wondered what determined who would ride below and who would ride above. I also wondered why on the happy occasion of going home, I felt so sad.

That was over forty years ago and none of my mates did I ever see again. As the song "Auld Lang Syne" says, we have truly run about in all directions and wandered many a weary mile while broad seas have roared between us.

But I haven't forgotten my mates of old long ago, for every so often they come to mind and I stop to make a toast to each of them:

To Dexter, my mate across the US, Japan, Korea, and then back to the US—mates for our entire military career.

To Ben, who I only knew in Japan and Korea. A friend to go down the river with, and always good for a dozen laughs. You still are, because I still chuckle when thinking of you.

To Ernst, who is probably a billionaire, but has to pay most of it out in alimony.

To Boy San, I hope and pray you found a real family.

To G.I. Joe, I hope you didn't live long in the sack you found yourself in.

To Mr. Ha, one of the most interesting people to whom I have ever spoken. I would now appreciate you much, much more.

To Big York, who is probably in the Australian outback helping Crocodile Dundee catch crocs.

To Buck and James, I am sorry you had to ride in the ship's deep dark belly and not topside with Dexter and me. I still wonder why. But anyway, here is to the good times we had.

To Terry, Wilson, Hill, and all the rest, here is to the good and bad times.

To Otsu, my crazy girl, you have a special place in my heart. You were an exciting trip. I sincerely hope you made it to the United States, and were able to explain the tattoo away to your husband's satisfaction.

To Namiko, my beautiful little Japanese princess, my teacher, my guru, my hero, the wind in my sails, you are all these things and much more.

Concerning my princess, we wrote to each other three times after our goodbye. Following is her last letter.

My dearest, my love, my very heart, separation has not dimmed my love for you in the least. It, in fact, grows stronger each day. I find it very hard to turn my thoughts from you in attending everyday things. It is so hard to push from mind your strong arms holding me while your gentle and soothing hands roam and caress. I can be sitting, standing, or walking, and still feel your body close to mine. I dream so often of us laying close together with my head on your shoulder. Sometimes, when in a crowd of noisy talking people, I am not there, but holding your hand as we walk along the rocky paths of my island. No, not mine, but our island, because in my heart you will always be here.

When I dare to walk up to our waterfall to do some painting, I feel you behind me watching. Any minute, I expect your arms to come about my waist, causing me to make a wrong brush stroke, and so wishing for the feel of them, not caring if I do make a bad brush stroke, willing to sacrifice the whole painting just to feel you for a second.

I often think of and feel the sensations of that cool morning we lay on our blanket by the waterfall: the cool breeze and the warm sun working together over our bodies giving us just the right comfort, with the falls sending just the right spray to us. That was perfect—two lovers lying close together, side by side, looking up at the sky watching the morning sunbeams breaking holes in the clouds and falling down through the tree branches. We needed nothing more. Life requires so little for happiness when it is flavored with love. I can see us now as if I am someone else looking on. I see two lovers so happy, so completely at peace, needing nothing but each other to be complete, two belonging together, two to make a whole. I see two lovers from opposite sides of the world, two lovers so different in culture and background, yet so tightly bound together by a love and bond that neither space nor time can break.

I know, my dearest heart, that I will always feel this way, because I always have. I loved you in the past, I love you now, I will love you forever. And I know that you love me just the same. You may not yet have come to believe it, but one day you will know that this is not our first love. Nor will it be our last.

I also know, as you do, that the time and place is wrong for us. Our families, our cultures, and especially the tragedy of my sister Isora are obstacles we see no way around. During our last days together you became aware of the pressure my family put on me to end our relationship and to act as an obedient Japanese lady should. Uncle Yoshiya seems determined to have me wed this nice Japanese man. But I am just as determined not to, not because he isn't a nice man. He is. But it wouldn't be fair. It wouldn't be fair to him or me, because I couldn't be a wife to him. I could only be a wife to you.

Aunt Mitchie is the only person to whom I can freely talk. She is so wise and understanding. She so completely understands our situation and has been such a help to me. You and she are the two people I most love. She knows this is my letter and doesn't want to impose but does want to tell you that you are special in her heart and always will be. She is helping me to rewrite my letter in English. I wanted it to be all in English so that you could read and understand it and not need Mr. Ha to translate it for you. We are composing this letter between our crying spells, so please forgive any smudges in the letters due to tear drops. It is the saddest letter I have ever written concerning the happiest days of my life.

I have discussed with Aunt Mitchie my situation in every detail concerning my love for you versus my family, my painting, Isora, and the Buddhist temple. As usual, Buddha has provided me with an answer.

I am to enter service with the Buddhist temple. There I can be of service to my people and will be allowed to see Isora when she needs me. I will not have to wed and still do honor to my family. I can pursue my studies and painting, and just as importantly, I can have uninterrupted thoughts of you.

So my Beautiful Big American Rebel, my American darling, this is my last letter, and since I will not be able to receive letters or visitors for a long while, let your answer be your last. I wish you a happy return home and many years of happiness. If it is willed that we never meet again in this life, remember that in my last breath, my thoughts will be of you. And thinking of that last breath is not an unpleasant thought, because then we will meet again.

Carl L. Poston Jr.

Your Little Japanese Princess,
Namiko

    I kept and treasured that letter along with her others for twenty-six years. Her last one I read so many times until I knew it by heart. Then on January 12,1981, they were destroyed in my office fire. Even though memorized, as years slipped by, it became a vague memory. Then one night recently as I lay sleeping and dreaming, I was abruptly awaken as if shaken. Then the contents of that letter stood in my memory as it had forty-four years ago. I got up at four AM and wrote it down, and I do believe it to be accurate almost word for word. For that letter to come to me like it did in the middle of the night puzzles me much. It makes me wonder if nothing ever leaves the mind, but is only stored away and subject to be pushed forward at any time. If so, what could have pushed it forth?
    Until the recall of this letter, I had nothing left of her except two not-so-good pictures and the pencil portrait she drew of me. Everything else was either lost in Korea or burned in my office fire. It is sad to have lost all the pictures and mementos of her; but really, who needs them with the memories I have? Who needs pictures when I can see her so clearly? Who needs pictures when I can see her long black hair blowing in the ocean breeze as she walks along the shore and her sparkling eyes as she looks at me smiling. What picture could allow me the feel of her soft and smooth, yet firm body next to mine, and let me savor the clean smell of her hair as I bury my face in it. What sort of picture would bring to my ears the sweet music of her laughter in happiness or her love sob in darkness?
    What is this thing that drives man so and makes the world go?
    What is it that drives him to accomplish all that he does—good and bad?
    What is this thing that makes him go when he wants to say no?
    What is it that drives him to be happy and sad?
    It is called woman.
    The driving power behind all of man's accomplishments—good or bad—happy or sad—is the love of a woman. Just to see her sway, or to hear her laughter in the day, or her whisper in the night, is enough to drive man as far as he can go.
    Without her, everything would stop, and without her, there could be no heaven.
    Our time together was short as time goes, but it touched my life with magic. It showed me what a glorious thing it is to love and be loved, and there is nothing I would exchange for that. However, there is a down side to it, because there is a big hole in my life where she used to be, which I have never been able to fill. Once having loved like that and lost, a man is never

really up to another love affair. Everyone is compared and too much is expected. So through the years, I drifted in and out of romances and marriages, always searching but never finding.

But life went on and as the years passed, her memory faded somewhat, and there were times she seldom came to mind. Then from nowhere and with no warning, her memory would come like a summer storm completely filling my mind and heart. However, she would only stay for a short while. It was like a short visit to make sure I didn't forget her.

But now in old age, she seems to come more often and to stay longer. And more and more I tend to believe as she did: this was not our first meeting nor will it be our last. Maybe our time is drawing near. Sometimes I feel anxious.

> I have been here before,
>   but when or how I cannot tell;
> I know the grass beyond the door,
>   the sweet keen smell,
> the sighing sound, the lights around the shore.
> <u>You have been mine before</u>—
>   how long ago I may not know:
> but just when at that swallow's soar
>   your neck turned so,
> some veil did fall—I knew it all of yore.

"Sudden Light"
Dante Gabriel Rossetti (1828-1882)